KATHLEEN.

A CHARMING LOVE STORY.

BY MRS. FRANCES HODGSON BURNETT.

AUTHOR OF

"THEO," "MISS ORESPIGNY," "A QUIET LIFE," "LINDSAY'S LUCK,"
"PRETTY POLLY PEMBERTON," "JARL'S DAUGHTER," ETC.

"KATHLEEN" is one of the most perfect and charming love stories ever published, tender, true and pathetic. Kathleen was a natural beauty, and made a decided impression on the heart of our hero long before she had learned the meaning of the word "LOVE." It was at a village on the coast of Maine, where she lived with her old grandmother, nine years before our story opens. Carl Seymour was an artist, and not rich when he met his love for the second time at Newport—met her to fall blindly at her feet, and worshipping her as all others did. But this second meeting was very different from the first; the old grandmother was dead, and Kathleen was chaperoned by a worldly-minded aunt, who had determined her niece should make a brilliant marriage. Carl Seymour proposed and was rejected. After three years of separation, in which time the aunt's money had taken wings, Kathleen reappears as the governess to Mrs. Armadale's children, a sister of Carl Seymour, in Mr. Seymour's house. Is it any wonder then that Carl Seymour and Kathleen, being thrown together thus, should forget all their past troubles, and that their cloud, which looked so black to both, had at the last so bright a silver lining! but we must refer the reader to the book itself. "KATHLEEN" is written in Mrs. Burnett's best mood, and is very pathetic.—*Critic.*

PHILADELPHIA:
T. B. PETERSON & BROTHERS;
306 CHESTNUT STREET.

MRS. BURNETT'S CHARMING NOVELETTES.

Kathleen. A Charming Love Story. *By Mrs. Frances Hodgson Burnett*, author of "Theo," "Miss Crespigny," "A Quiet Life," "Pretty Polly Pemberton," "Lindsay's Luck," and "Jarl's Daughter."

"Theo." A Sprightly Love Story. *By Mrs. Frances Hodgson Burnett*, author of "Kathleen," "Pretty Polly Pemberton," "Miss Crespigny," "A Quiet Life," "Lindsay's Luck," and "Jarl's Daughter."

Pretty Polly Pemberton. A Charming Love Story. *By Mrs. Frances Hodgson Burnett*, author of "Theo," "Kathleen," "A Quiet Life," "Miss Crespigny," "Lindsay's Luck," and "Jarl's Daughter."

Miss Crespigny. A Powerful Love Story. *By Mrs. Frances Hodgson Burnett*, author of "Theo," "Kathleen," "A Quiet Life," "Pretty Polly Pemberton," "Lindsay's Luck," and "Jarl's Daughter."

Lindsay's Luck. A Fascinating Love Story. *By Mrs. Frances Hodgson Burnett*, author of "Theo," "Kathleen," "A Quiet Life," "Miss Crespigny," "Jarl's Daughter," and "Pretty Polly Pemberton."

A Quiet Life: and The Tide on the Moaning Bar. Tender and Pathetic Stories. *By Mrs. Frances Hodgson Burnett*, author of "Theo," "Kathleen," "Miss Crespigny," "Pretty Polly Pemberton," "Lindsay's Luck," and "Jarl's Daughter."

Jarl's Daughter; and Other Novelettes. *By Mrs. Frances Hodgson Burnett*, author of "Theo," "Kathleen," "A Quiet Life," "Pretty Polly Pemberton," "Lindsay's Luck," and "Miss Crespigny."

Above are 50 cents each in paper cover, or $1.00 each in cloth, black and gold.

CONTENTS.

(20)

KATHLEEN.

BY MRS. FRANCES HODGSON BURNETT

AUTHOR OF

"THEO," "MISS CRESPIGNY," "A QUIET LIFE," "LINDSAY'S LUCK,"
"PRETTY POLLY PEMBERTON," "JARL'S DAUGHTER," ETC.

CHAPTER I.

CIRCE.

"THERE she goes!" said Fayne, "on that light-built black. Jove! how she rides!"

All the men rushed to the window, as men will rush, to look at a feminine celebrity. Three of them there were—Brandon, Coyne, and Meynell. Fayne had a place in the window before. One man had not moved—that man was Carl Seymour; and belles were not his hobby, so he kept his seat and went on sketching.

"She," who was properly represented by Kate Davenant, passed by the Ocean House on a dashing trot, her groom following her; and when she was out of sight, the men came back to their seats again. (21)

"I wonder if it's true?" said Brandon, half hesitatingly.

"If what is true?" asked Fayne.

"About— Well, they say she is such a dreadful flirt, you know. She don't look like it."

Carl Seymour shrugged his shoulders.

"Don't be so guileless, my dear fellow," he said. "Women never do 'look like it.' Innocence is their chief characteristic. Do you suppose Eve 'looked like it' when she gave Adam the apple? No! If she had done, the masculine part of humanity, at least, would have been rusticating in the Garden of Eden to the present day."

"Have you ever met her?" asked Coyne, suddenly.

"Eve? No, not to my recollection."

"Miss Davenant, I mean?"

"No."

"Well," said Coyne, with an odd tone in his voice, "don't form any opinion until you have. You might be sorry afterward. Older men than you have risked their whole happiness upon that woman; wiser and as cool-headed men (I don't think there are many cooler-headed) would have given their lives for a smile from her lips." And he walked to the window with his hands in his pockets, and began to whistle softly. A little silence followed, one of those unaccountable silences which, sometimes, fall upon talkers with an odd sense of present discomfort or warning for the future.

Coyne was the oldest of the party, who were spending the summer at Newport. Kate Davenant had been the last arrival, and as she was a woman, and beautiful, she had been pretty liberally discussed. Perhaps the discussion had been all the more liberal, because Miss Davenant's fame had reached Newport before her. People, the stronger sex more especially, had a great deal to say about Miss Davenant. About her perfection of beauty, in the first place; about her wonderful magnetic fascination; about the tastefulness of her toilets; and last, but not least, about her aunt and chaperon, Mrs. Mortimer Montgomery. The latter lady was certainly all that society could desire as an indorsement. Rich, well-born, a leader of the ton in New York, her right to rule supreme was not to be disputed. But that did not account for Miss 'Davenant. Some bold inquirer had once ventured to ask about Kate, but had been decidedly snubbed, for Mrs. Mortimer Montgomery had merely placed her eyeglass in her aristocratic eye and stared her down, saying, " Kate is my adopted daughter," and from that day the irrepressible member had been " cut." So the matter rested, when Miss Davenant made her first appearance at Newport. Her costumes were superb pieces of art, her air was perfect, the witchery of her manner carried all before it. She might be the heiress of millions, even of billions, or she might be merely a dependent upon Mrs. Mortimer Montgomery—a poor relation—but to some people the uncertainty made the situation all the more piquant.

"George!" ejaculated young Spooney, who was an unsung hero on the lookout for a fortune, "it's like a lottery, jolly, but dangerous. Fellow puts down his money, and draws either a prize or a blank."

Now I will go back to the men who helped me to open my story.

Brandon, Fayne, and Meynell have gone to play billiards. Coyne and Seymour have stayed behind. The man with the clear eyes, straight features, and down-drooping blond moustache, is Carl Seymour: the dark-faced man who leans upon the window is Angus Coyne.

"I remember just such an evening as this spent by the sea-side, nine—no, ten years ago," said Seymour, and he broke off with a short, half-forced laugh.

Coyne looked up at him.

"What," he said, "have you a romance, too?"

Seymour laughed again.

"Yes. The oldest of all romances. A romance with a nine-year-old heroine."

"A romance, indeed," said Coyne. "But how did it become one?"

Seymour threw himself into an arm-chair, and looked out at the sea again with something of thought in his face.

"There are strange things in a man's life," he said, musingly. "I often look back on mine, and wonder at the changing path that leads us all to the one ending—a mound of earth covering all our old faults and stumblings. There has been plenty of change in mine, but only one romance, and Miss Davenant and the sea brought it back to me to-night."

"Miss Davenant?"

"Yes. Kate Davenant you said: and a Kate, or Kathleen, was my little heroine. Wait a moment, you shall see her."

He went to his desk and brought out a package of drawings, laying them before his friend.

"Look at her," he said, with a glow in his eyes. "The little darling! Kathleen Mavourneen, I used to call her."

There were about a dozen rough pictures, some larger, some smaller, some half-finished, some perfect, and colored; but all taken from one model. A slender, wild-looking child, with great stars of eyes, and wonderful tangled hair. The prettiest, and most perfect of all, was colored, and showed her standing, barefooted and bare-headed, ankle-deep in the tide, picking up shells; her cheeks all abloom, her magnificent unkempt hair blown out like a flame-colored banner, and tossing over her shoulders.

"That was the first time I saw her," commented Carl. "It was at a little village on the coast of Maine, where she lived with her old grandmother. Nine years ago," with a half sigh. "How time flies!"

"She is a weird-looking little beauty," said Coyne, "but how did your story end?"

"Practically. Perhaps a little sadly, too. It ended with my good-bys, and with Kathleen's arms round my neck, and her tawny mane blowing in my eyes as she kissed me. No woman has kissed me since—sometimes I think no woman ever will. 'Kathleen Mavourneen' spoiled me for the rest of womankind."

"Don't let her prove fatal to your happiness," jested Coyne. "Kates are dangerous; and do you know, this child-love of yours is not unlike that most dangerous of all Kates—Kate Davenant?"

"I hope not," said Seymour, quickly. "I would rather think not."

"Why not?" asked Coyne, as quickly. "You say you have never seen her?"

"No; and I don't know why, unless that I want to keep my little Kathie to myself. I don't want to hear men speak of her as they speak of Miss Davenant. It may seem absurd and romantic to you, but I think if ever I saw Kate Ogilvie again, I should make her my wife; and I don't wish to think men have made bets on my wife's flirtations, and called her the Circe."

Coyne did not answer. He was thinking of Kathleen Mavourneen—not Seymour's, but Kathleen Mavourneen, as Kate Davenant had sung it to him, a few months ago, in the old-fashioned hotel-garden on the banks of the Rhine; for Kate and her aunt had just come back from a tour of two years in Europe. Kate Davenant had been his romance. Had been, I say, because the romance was over now, and he had only been one of the many whom men had made bets about; only one of the many who had succumbed to the charming of the woman they called the Circe.

CHAPTER II.

LOVE HAS THORNS.

ON an elegant little stand, in a charming dressing-room, stood a bouquet of scarlet and white blossoms, fringed with feathery grasses : and opposite the stand, sitting in a luxurious arm-chair, lounged Kate Davenant.

Kate Davenant! It could be no other. Look at her! Slender, rounded limbs; face like snow, with a soft rose-red palpitating on either cheek ; eyes dark and brilliant; great masses of brown, satiny hair, that, in some lights, looked almost black. She wore a white morning-dress, with open sleeves, that showed the beautifully rounded arm; and in the bosom of the dress were some fresh flowers. Her attitude was pensive: and yet one hardly realized that so gay and bright a countenance could be pensive, even for a moment. The artistic light, falling upon her artistic face; her small, arched feet, in their pretty slippers; the easy, graceful lines of the half-lounging figure—what a picture it was! Suddenly she jumped from the chair, and went to the cheval glass. She glanced at herself, from arching foot to shining, delicate head, just as a critical observer might look at a beautiful picture. There was something in her eyes that seemed a little like fascination, as she drew nearer and nearer, until the bright, morning sunshine, falling full upon her, brought out all the brilliancy of rose-red and dazzling white on her skin. She gazed at it all for a few moments, and then her lips parted in an oddly scornful, ungirlish laugh.

"What is it all worth?" she said. "The outline is graceful, the tinting rich and delicate. What will it bring, I wonder? But the picture goes to the highest bidder, of course."

It was so bitterly said, that the very energy seemed to rouse her from her late languid mood. She rang for her maid.

"Lotte," she said, when the girl came in, "where did those flowers come from?" and she pointed to the bouquet upon the stand.

"Mr. Griffith sent them. They arrived this morning early."

Miss Davenant shrugged her shoulders.

"Where is Mrs. Montgomery?"

"In her room. There was a note, ma'amselle, with the flowers."

"That will do."

When the girl was gone, she took the note in her hand and read it with the little oddly sarcastic smile curving her lips.

"Very pretty, Mr. Griffith!" shrugging her shoulders again. "Very pretty indeed—but is it wise? Do you know how many people send bouquets and make these charming speeches? Nevertheless, since you desire it—" She stopped, and taking a waxen camelia from the cluster, put it in a small glass by itself. "There, it will keep fresher now, and I will wear it this evening," she said.

Three years ago there would have been a little pang of remorse in her heart; for this poor Tom Griffith, who sent the flowers, was an honest young fellow, and loved her as only an honest-hearted simpleton can love a woman who was such a woman as Kate Davenant was. "The Circe," the men called her. Well, well, when a woman loses her faith in the world, God help her, and mankind pity her, I say! Kate Davenant had lost her faith long ago. Perhaps, as I tell my story, you will understand how she had lost it; but now I can only show her to you as a woman, whose wonderful grace and beauty turned the great game of hearts into her hands, and brought new excitement into her half frothed-out life.

"What has the world done for me?" she asked herself, bitterly, a thousand times. "There may be love and truth in it, but I have not seen it yet, heaven help me!"

So it was that she wore Tom Griffith's flower that night, with a little sarcastic remembrance of how many flowers she had worn before, and how many flowers she had flung aside as soon as she tired of them.

She went down to Mrs. Montgomery after she was dressed, and found that aristocratic matron in a humor which was none of the best. "It's perfectly absurd!" said her aunt. "I came here to escape Brown, Jones, and Robinson, and no sooner do I find a comfortable parlor in a hotel, than Brown, Jones, and Robinson make an invasion. I thought Newport was select, but in the present state of society no place is select. One runs against Brown in Paris, meets Jones in full costume on Mount Blanc, and has Robinson staring one in the face at the Tuilleries. I will tell you what I have been thinking of, Kate. I saw, yesterday, in our drive, that a handsome house was to be let down the avenue. Why shouldn't we take it for the season?"

"We might," said Miss Davenant. "I for one am tired of hotel life."

Mrs. Mortimer Montgomery looked meditatively for a moment.

"We will," she said, at last. "One feels so much more at ease in a private establishment."

Mrs. Montgomery was a decisive, business-like woman, and her "We will" was conclusive; so, that point disposed of, she turned her attention to another.

"Where did you get your flowers from?" she asked.

Kate glanced indolently at the reflected blossoms in the pier-glass, and smiled a little.

"From Mr. Griffith."

Her aunt put her eye-glass to her eye, and coughed somewhat reprovingly.

"Very good, my dear. And Mr.—Mr.—this young man, whatever his name is, got them at the florist's, and paid a ruinous price for the pleasure of seeing you wear them. You are a very handsome woman, Kate—but don't you think that sort of thing may be carried too far?"

Kate shrugged her shoulders with a little haughty, indifferent gesture. She did not like interference, even from her aunt.

"My dear aunt," she said, "I wear the green ticket yet, you know, and as a wearer of the green ticket am entitled to a little amusement. I am very wicked, of course, and 'this sort of thing' is very shocking; but then, you see, wouldn't life be a trifle wearing without it? Our life, I mean. We don't look forward to domestic felicity, and the days of Arcadian shepherds and shepherdesses lie a few centuries behind us."

Her aunt's reply was very laconic. She never entered into discussion.

"You please yourself, of course," she said. "My remark was a mere suggestion. I don't think there is any fear of your getting romantic notions, at least."

The following day, Mrs. Montgomery proceeded to make arrangements connected with her new establishment, and within a week she took possession, with the full intent of enjoying herself.

"If I like the place as much as ever at the end of the season, I will buy it," she said to Kate.

A few days later, as Miss Davenant sat at the piano, her aunt came in from making some calls.

"You remember the Scotchman we met in Germany, Kate?" she asked. "Coyne, his name was."

Kate's hands dropped away from the keys, and her face caught an expression of faint interest.

"Yes. What reminded you of him?"

"I met him to-day at the Farnhams. He came with a friend to call on Alice. The friend was quite a striking-

2

looking man.   His name was Carl Seymour, and he is an
artist."

" Carl Seymour, did you say ? "

" Yes.   What a pity such men should be thrown into
such places!   I told them they might call on us.   Where
is Lotte?   I want her."

When her relative had gone in search of Lotte, Kate
Davenant got up from the piano and walked to the hearth,
resting both elbows on the mantle, and looking at herself.
There was a brief space, in which the beautiful face the
pier-glass reflected was quite clear to her sight; but, then,
something strangely like tears blurred the reflection with
their mist, and at last she dropped her face with a little
rising tremor in her throat.   Tears did not come easily
into Kate Davenant's eyes; but now the fresh breath of
sea air blowing through the open window, mingled itself
with an old memory of childish days, so much purer and
better than her womanhood, that her eyes filled in spite
of all.

" I wonder if he has forgotten?   Men forget these
things more easily than women.   But, ah, me! nine
years—nine years, and ' Kathleen Mavourneen' is a woman
of the world."

When Coyne and Seymour returned from their call

upon Alice Farnham, they talked about Mrs. Montgomery and her niece.

"I may be a fool!" said Coyne, with his gray eyes flashing. "I may be a fool, but I do not forget her—I never can!"

In their room they found Tom Griffith waiting for them, evidently in a very ecstatic frame of mind.

"I've been to Mrs. Mortimer Montgomery's," he said. "Kate—Miss Davenant—has promised to drive out with me this evening;" and he glanced down rather sheepishly at a rose in his button-hole.

Carl seated himself before his easel and began to work, whistling the while softly. Was there never a man yet who had resisted Kate Davenant's witchery? He had never heard of one: and in a half-angered wonder at her fascination, he felt a certain haughty power to resist it himself.

It was weeks before he saw her. Newport grew gayer and gayer, and Mrs. Montgomery's entertainments were the principal features in its gayety. Kate rode by the hotel every day, sometimes with one adorer, sometimes with another, and sometimes only with a groom; but Seymour never cared to look up. The men brought stories of her, and grew loud in their admiration of her grace; and every man who spoke of her was one added to the list of victims.

But, at last, a sensation arose in the shape of croquet-parties, and at the first of these assemblies Carl met the syren. The party was given at the Farnhams; and when he made his appearance, pretty, good-natured Alice took possession of him, and proceeded to enlighten him as to various members of the company.

"The gentleman with the dark face is the new nabob, Mr. Collier, and that tall gentleman is our literary lion, Gerald Colycinth; and the one standing near him is a senator. It takes all sorts of people to make up a croquet-party; but one must have a sprinkling of celebrities, you know. Now, I want to show you somebody very important. Let me see—where is she? But of course, you have seen Miss Davenant—the Circe, as they call her?"

"Not, 'of course,'" said Carl, "because I have not yet had that pleasure."

Alice's blue eyes flew open.

"Is it possible? Why, every one is going crazy about her."

"Pray, except me," replied Carl, with mock gravity. "I am anxious to preserve my senses."

"Wait until you know her," laughed Alice. "Ah! there she is. The centre of attraction of that knot of gentlemen. They always *do* crowd around her in that manner, celebrities and all. It is my impression the senator would give his seat for a smile. How does she manage to dress so perfectly?"

As Alice said, Kate was, as usual, the centre of attraction of a knot of the enslaved. Carl looked at her, and fairly caught his breath. He was an artist, and the wonderful perfection of tinting in wearer and costume struck him with an intense pleasure. Some world-reading Frenchwoman has said: "Give me a handsome pair of eyes, and I will do the rest." Kate Davenant had not only the eyes, but every other beauty; and then she thoroughly understood what the Frenchwoman spoke of as "the rest." Dress is a rather powerful attraction, and in this age of improvements beauty unadorned would be quite likely to be pronounced a dowdy. Keeping this in mind, Miss Davenant ruled supreme. Of her dress, I will only say that it was a wonderful piece of art, and from satiny puffs to slender foot a charming blending of delicate pearl-gray lace and flowers.

"Charmed already?" jested Alice, looking at Carl's watching face.

He shook his head.

"No. I am thinking of something. Do you remember the poem?

> "'As you sit where lustres strike you,
>   Sure to please,
>   Do we love you most, or like you,
>   Belle Marquise?'"

Alice tapped the tip of her slim slipper meditatively with her mallet. She was a nice girl, but her good-nature did not make her very fond of Kate Davenant. A woman who is a belle is very rarely a favorite with her own sex— and Miss Davenant's success was too universal to make the feminine darlings absolutely adore her; and apart from that, Alice Farnham had a small thorn on her own account in the shape of Tom Griffith. Tom Griffith was her cousin, and until lately something a little more; but circumstances alter cases, and this case, the Circe had altered herself, and doing so had not gained pretty Alice's fervent esteem. Accordingly, the young lady did not defend her against Seymour's quotation.

CHAPTER III.

AN OLD ACQUAINTANCE.

MISS DAVENANT went through her croquet, as she went through everything else, with gracefulness and success. The people who looked upon the game scientifically were charmed with her interest and knowledge of its points ; and those who regarded it merely as a game found time to be charmed with her beautiful face and spirited comments. Once or twice, during the evening, she glanced towards Carl Seymour with a quick searching in her eyes.

"Who is he?" she asked of Tom Griffith, as she sent the senator's ball spinning across the lawn. "The slender man, with the blond moustache, I mean."

"Don't you know him?" asked Tom, a little surprised. "That's Carl Seymour."

"An artist, is he not?" said Kate, coolly. "Mind where you send that ball."

"Yes. Painted 'Ulysses and the Syrens'—that picture there was such a furore about."

"I remember. Quite a celebrity, I should imagine," and she went on with her croquet.

Half a dozen times in the course of the afternoon, Carl Seymour passed her, and always with such a cool, careless face, that she could not fail to notice it—another woman might have been annoyed. Not so Kate Davenant. She knew better than to feel displeasure at an indifference which she was certain to overcome. Perhaps it pleased her a little. At any rate, it piqued her curiously. But, at last, on his way to recover a truant ball, Carl passed her as she stood in a little knot of admirers, laughing. There was a wonderful silver tone in her laughter, and something in it struck Carl Seymour, when he heard it, with an odd sense of remembrance. Where had he heard the laugh before? Then he turned and looked at her face. His glance did not seem to trouble her; the fringed, purple eyes swept him from head to foot, and then Miss Davenant took up the thread of her conversation. He had never seen such eyes as those but once before; and his memory went back to the rock-bound shore, and the sweet child-face, so like, yet so unlike this girl's—the face of the child-love he had called Kathleen Mavourneen.

He stood at some little distance listening to her and looking at her. The rose-red fluttered on her cheek, and the soft, large eyes opened and drooped. The usually grave senator gazed at the fair face entranced, and listened for

every ring of her sweet laugh, as he would have listened
for the notes of a prima-donna. There was a curious con-
test going on in Carl Seymour's mind. He was wondering
whether Miss Davenant attracted or repelled him. The
sweet flower-face struck every artistic taste; the memory
in the silver laugh touched him he knew not how; but
then again came a remembrance of the stories he had
heard, stories which to a proud, fastidious man seemed
almost terrible. It might be a beautiful woman who wore
Tom Griffith's flowers, and dazzled proud men with her
smiles: but was it a true one! Others might have been
content with the rose-leaf tints and star eyes. Carl Seymour was not. He was a man apt to be a little sarcastic
and severe upon women of the world; and as he watched
Kate Davenant, he thought of the marquise again, and
wondered if the application was not correct:

"You are just a porcelain trifle,
Belle Marquise;
Just a thing of puffs and patches,
Made for madrigals and catches,
Not for heart-wounds, but for scratches,
Oh, Marquise!

"Just a pinky porcelain trifle,
Belle Marquise;

Pate tendre, rose Du Barry,
Quick at verbal point and parry;
Clever, certes—but to marry—
    No, Marquise!"

He was thinking over this as Miss Davenant chatted
with the enamored senator, and laughed musically at poor
Tom Griffith's somewhat far-fetched witticisms. He was
thinking about it when, at last, she took the senator's
arm, and came toward Carl's side of the lawn.

He was an elderly bachelor, this senator; and, like
most elderly bachelors, quite susceptible, and felt more
than senatorial dignity as he crossed the ground with the
exquisitely gloved hand resting upon his portly arm, and
Kate's voice softened deferentially. One of the fair hands
was ungloved, and after the trailing dress had swept by
him, glancing downward, Carl Seymour caught sight of a
delicately-tinted trifle of pearl-gray glove lying at his feet.
He took it up. Such a trifle as it was! Such a very
bijou of kid and silver-thread embroidery! Just with the
very moulding of the soft fingers, with the very faint
fragrance of lilies floating over it. Carl smiled a little
with a half sensation of pleasure, it was so pretty. A few
steps took him to Miss Davenant's side, and a few words
attracted her attention.

"Pardon me!" he said, bowing. "But you have dropped your glove."

Just a faint flutter of red on her cheek as she took it from his hand, just a soft uplifting of the dark-fringed eyes.

"I thank you!" she said, returning his bow, and then she passed him.

Only two words, and such simple ones; but it was the Circe who had uttered them, and in the sweet, sweet voice which had touched so many hearts before. It had hardly occupied a minute's time; and when she passed on, she seemed to have forgotten it, and the voice that addressed the senator was just as sweet. Nevertheless, Carl felt a little spell-bound, in spite of his sarcasm. He forgot about the marquise, and stood still looking after her.

"I don't wonder at their calling her the Circe," he said. And then the old memory came back to him, and he added lowly, though smiling at his fancy, "Kathleen Mavourneen! Kathleen Mavourneen!"

As he stood there, he saw an elderly lady coming from the house, leaning on a gentleman's arm. A once handsome woman, perhaps a belle in her time, but just now suggestive of a dowager, in the sere and yellow leaf, and at the same time a woman with a great deal of haughtiness in her carriage, and cool speculation in her keen, handsome eyes. He knew who it was. He had seen Mrs. Mortimer Montgomery before, and guessed rightly that she intended to renew her acquaintance with him. Mrs. Montgomery understood precisely how much a celebrity was worth in the fashionable world, and "Ulysses and the Syrens" had done a great deal toward earning Carl Seymour a name.

She stopped on reaching him, and introduced her companion, the gentleman who Alice Farnham had spoken of as our "literary lion."

"Lions, both of you!" she said, nodding her handsome old head. "How is it that you have not been roaring this evening, Mr. Seymour? When we are so fortunate as to secure a lion in our menagerie of society, we consider ourselves cheated if he don't exhibit his leonine characteristics."

"But I am such a very young lion," laughed Carl. "Quite a cub, one might say. And wouldn't my roar be a little too mild among the full-grown quadrupeds?"

Mrs. Montgomery laughed, too. She liked men who were apt and self-possessed—and this gentleman seemed to be both.

"You are too modest," she said. "But I must not

forget what I came here for. Why don't you call on us? Kate saw your picture last season, and has been talking about it ever since. Art and artists are her hobby. She has been collecting gems for the last three years."

Carl smilingly accepted the invitation. Fate had certainly taken him in hand, and Fate rules us all. When Mrs. Montgomery carried her lion back to the house, she also carried Carl's promise that he would call upon her the next day.

"Kate will be delighted to see you," she said, with the smiling nod. "Good-evening!"

After that my hero went over to Alice Farnham, and chatted with her until the company dispersed, and then he returned home and looked at the picture of little Kathie, wondering at the resemblance between the two pairs of tender eyes.

Eleven the next morning found him at Mrs. Montgomery's. He had sent up his card, and was waiting her appearance. He looked round the room carelessly. Traces of "Kate" here and there—in the pretty work-table, on which lay an open book with a filmy handkerchief flung upon its pages, and in the pearl card-case, with a tasseled glove lying by it—the very glove he had picked up the

day before. He saw it, and smiled. There were many
paintings hung against the walls, and suddenly one of
them catching his eye, he rose, uttering an exclamation
of surprise. It was a very small picture, but its frame
was heavy and rich in the extreme, and the subject a little
weird and wild—just a strip of rocky shore, with gray,
tossing waves sweeping into a little cove, and heavy, purple clouds glowering above. Spirited, very, and perfect
both in outline and coloring. Evidently the work of no
unpractised hand.

But it was not this which had given rise to Seymour's
exclamation. The scene was the most familiar of the
many connected with the by-gone romance. It was the
little bay, on the coast of Maine, where Kathie's red cloak
had always been his signal among the rocks. When Mrs.
Montgomery entered, he was still standing before the
painting; and after the first salutations were over, he
began to question her.

"May I ask where it came from?" he said. "I thought
no one knew that spot but myself."

"Kate painted it," replied her ladyship, a thought indifferently. "She is always dashing off some little wild
scene or other. I don't know where she gets them from.
Ah, Kate! here you are to answer for yourself."

Miss Davenant had just opened the door, and stood before them with a great bunch of red roses in her hand. She came forward and laid them on the table, and on her aunt's introduction, extended her hand with the old charming smile. She was glad to meet Mr. Seymour. She had made his acquaintance by reputation long ago. How could picture-lovers thank him for "Ulysses and the Syrens?" There was nothing of effect in her manner, nothing of ancestry to produce an impression. Simply the grace and elegance of a graceful and elegant woman of the world, who desired to please, and knew how to do it. Witching deference enslaved the senator, her face alone was enough for Tom Griffith, but Carl Seymour stood apart from other men, and she only helped Fate a little with her tender eyes and exquisite voice.

"I have been asking your aunt about this painting," said Seymour, at last. "She tells me you are the artist. It cannot possibly be a fancy picture?"

She looked up at it smiling.

"No," she said. "It is a scene from memory. It was my home once."

Seymour was almost angry with himself for the wild supposition which flashed upon him. And yet the coincidence was so odd. He glanced at the slim hand upon

which the sunlight struck whitely, upon the brown, burnished hair, and then at the clear-cut, flawless face. Only
the large, heavily-fringed eyes held anything of remembrance for him. The rest was beautiful, but that was all.
The subject dropped quietly.

He listened to the soft voice as she talked to him with
perfect grace in every word and tone, and as he listened,
wondered if the same spell lay upon other men as lay
upon him. It was not such a spell as he had imagined it
to be—not the witchery of a coquette; something finer,
something more like the subtle instinct of a fair woman
who has seen the world, and understanding it, still retains
her tender sweetness. In this lay the secret of Kate
Davenant's success. Every man forgot, in her presence,
that other men had seen the same smiles, and heard the
same musical inflections of her voice. Carl Seymour
forgot this, too. It was hard to realize that such eyes as
these could be false; that of this stately, fair-faced girl
people had said: "There are men whom her beauty and
vanity have driven to worse than death." I am telling a
story frankly, and will not professs to hide that Carl Seymour was a better man than Kate Davenant was a woman.
The influences upon their lives had been different. The
one had seen purity and honor, the other worldliness and

the world. So it was that it was easier for Carl Seymour to believe that he had deceived himself, than to believe that the woman who seemed true could be deceiving him. That he was bitter against worldliness, I have told you, but the memory of a stately, womanly mother, and a true, pure-hearted little sister, in his far-away home, made him readier to be merciful than he would otherwise have been. Kate Davenant, too, was, perhaps, a little truer to herself to-day than she generally was—for there were old memories thrilling her as she watched his handsome, cavalier face.

She showed him the collection of art-pets, of which Mrs. Montgomery had spoken. Forgetting the Circe in her natural pleasure at his familiarity with, and interest in them, she lost herself in her animation, and stood with uplifted eyes and soft, rose-red on her cheek, as he warmed into enthusiasm over the art he loved so well. She had seen the grand master-pieces of which he spoke, and knew them as well as he did; but there were subtle, tender touches in their grandeur and beauty which she had dreamed of vaguely, but which grew into great, glowing truths under his warmth and eloquence. Carl turned upon her suddenly once, and saw something of this earnestness in her face. Years ago he had seen the same

3

rapt expression before, and its reproduction made him catch his breath with a swift heart-throb.

Mrs. Montgomery was delighted. This was a lion to boast of; and when he left them, her invitations were even more cordial than before.

"Kate," she said, when the door had closed behind him, "that man is a genius. What a pity he is so abominably poor. Mr. Coyne tells me he has absolutely nothing to depend upon but his art. If it was not for his circumstances, I should say he was exactly the man you ought to marry."

Miss Davenant was toying with a red rose, and she tore it into two pieces, slowly and deliberately, before she gave her answer.

"I don't think he is. Mr. Seymour is a truthful, honest man, and I am not a truthful, honest woman. Besides, as you intimate, intellect and honor are not marketable qualities." And she tossed the rose from her with a little impatient, disgusted gesture, and taking her coral-case from the table, left Mrs. Montgomery alone to her meditations.

Her aunt shrugged her shoulders.

Below, another incident occurred. As Seymour passed through the hall, he caught sight of a blood-red rose lying upon the floor. It had dropped from the handful Kate Davenant had brought into the drawing-room, and because of this he stooped and picked it up. He hardly knew his reason at the time, but long after he remembered it, and remembered, too, the little thrill that passed through him as its rich fragrance floated upward.

CHAPTER IV.

FROM DAY-DREAMS TO WAKING.

AFTER this first visit, there came some change into Carl Seymour's manner of living. The world saw more of him, and heard more of him, too, for Mrs. Montgomery sounded the praises of her pet-lion far and wide. People liked him, this poor, proud young artist, and courted him in spite of his poverty.

Women liked his handsome face, and were glad to see it everywhere; even liked his high-bred geniality, and were glad to meet him. Select society came to see the pictures in his rooms, and one or two connoisseurs made flattering comments on them. He had not come to New-port, like the rest of mankind, for recreation; he had come to take advantage of the peculiar scenery, and he worked hard with a cool sort of immovable energy. In his working hours he contracted a habit of sketching Kate Davenant's face on scraps of paper, and then tearing them up with a half-sneering wonder if he were as weak as the rest. There was a small bust of Clytie on his mantel-piece—a delicate, pure-faced head, with shoulders rising from the cup of a lily; and this star-faced Clytie he had bought because he fancied it was like Kate Davenant. There was the same soft droop of the lips, the same delicately-moulded chin and throat, and the same rich, curving ripple on the hair—the curving ripple one always sees on the heads of Greek statuary. He used to stop and look at it sometimes when he was tired, gaining something of inspiration from the calm, snowy face. In society he met Miss Davenant often, and a little instinct of half-recognized familiarity grew up between them. It was a dangerous position he was in, and all the more so, because he was unconscious of its danger. He thought it was only her beauty that attracted him so. He thought his bitterness against the faults people assigned to her would save him and keep him strong; he thought anything and everything but the truth, and so blindly allowed the current of events to sweep him onward to the general vortex.

Mrs. Montgomery had taken a wonderful fancy to him, and exhibited her preference as she never exhibited preference for others. When she met him in society, she would offer him a seat at her side, and give him the full benefit of her experience, talking to him with an odd brilliance, and apt sarcasm, which was truthful and world-reading beyond measure.

"I like men who have their fortunes to carve out," she said, on one occasion, laying her handsome hand on his shoulder as she looked at a picture that rested upon his easel. "I am tired of people who are born with the silver spoon. Kate is just such a woman as you are a man."

Carl laughed a little, and asked how Miss Davenant was like him.

"In her manner of thinking," said Mrs. Montgomery; "and in her haughtiness and self-reliance. Not that she shows her characteristics. She is too fond of popularity for that, and society keeps her within bounds."

And so Kate was fond of popularity and admiration. Carl thought of "*la belle marquise*" again, and forgot to look at the Clytie once that day. But in the evening he called upon Miss Davenant. He had not intended to do it at first; but when his stroll brought him opposite Bay View, he changed his mind, and concluded to make the visit There was a quaintly-carved balcony before the back drawing-room window, and Kate had stepped out upon it, and was watching the sun setting over the low hills toward the fort. She did not know that Seymour had entered. She wore a thin, vaprous white dress, and ruches of delicate white lace closed round throat and wrists. A great golden-hearted lily rested against the thick, dark puffs of her hair, and the last vivid shower of sunbeam floated round her in a light which was almost misty in its intensity. She was bending forward, leaning upon the balustrade, and looking out far away, as if she had forgotten herself. Her lips were a little parted, her eyes softly dilated.

The same weariness rested upon her red lips, with a bitter curve, that said a great deal to the man who watched her. Little Kathleen's face had never been so sad as this; but in some way, he felt as if he were near her now. What was she thinking of? This was not the woman men called the Circe. He stood in unobserved silence for a while, and then some unintentional movement attracted her attention, and she started and turned toward him. Then it was that he saw what he had not observed before. There were unshed tears in her eyes: the fringing lashes were quite wet. One moment she was half embarrassed, but the next she recovered herself, and came forward with extended hand, comparatively self-possessed, but still not entirely herself.

"I beg pardon," she said, smilingly. "I did not know you were here. I was watching the sunset, and sentimentalizing, thinking of a scrap of poetry I have somewhere seen.

"'The golden sunset shed
    Its glory o'er the sea; ·
    The dreams of earlier youth come back,
      Come back to me.'"

He glanced down at her, wondering a little.

"Such thoughts come to us all, sometimes," he said. "And, perhaps, these softened moments redeem some few of our past sins."

"Yes," she said, dreamily, looking toward the sunset again. "I was thinking how full our lives are of useless longing and vain regret. I was thinking that if I could only be a little child again—if I could only be a little child again—" her voice broke off in a sigh, which was half a sob. Then she began again suddenly: "I dare say you think I am weary; but after the first freshness is worn off, the world is—the world, you know; and profit and loss becomes the rule we worldlings calculate by. I was thinking about this when you came, and—forgot myself. I am glad it was you who surprised me, Mr. Seymour," with a soft, frank laugh, "and not my aunt. I am not often sentimental, but when I am, I don't wish my matter-of-fact relative to witness the demonstration."

Carl smiled a little. He could understand that feeling easily.

"You wish to be a child again," he said, after a silence. "May I ask you where your childhood was spent?"

Her color deepened.

"Yes," she said, at last, in a low voice. "The little picture, which interested you so, was one of the most familiar scenes of my childhood. I spent, at least, nine years of my life there."

"I am glad to hear it," said Carl. "It happens, strange to say, to be the scene of the one romance of my life."

"Mr. Coyne told me about it," said Miss Davenant, hurriedly. "Poor little Kathleen!"

"Why, 'poor little Kathleen?'" he asked, scanning her curiously. "She was a very happy child in those days."

"But she must be a woman now. Let me see—as old as I am. Imagine your little charmer a fisherman's or sailor's wife, with a stentorian voice! Did you love her, Mr. Seymour?"

The first part of her sentence had been light and jesting, the last seemed the result of sudden impulse, and her sweet voice sunk almost tremulously as she asked the question. All the blood in Carl Seymour's body seemed to rush to his heart. Doubt and certainty had been battling in his mind, and at the last speech, doubt seemed almost wholly overruled.

"Love her?" he said, with something like passion in his voice. "Love her? I love her still. My pure-hearted, innocent little Kathleen was the first love of my life: sometimes I think she will be the last."

Miss Davenant made no reply at first, but after a silence, she spoke again, as if meditatively.

"I am glad you have not forgotten her. I like to think some one has loved her truly. Poor, lonely little Kathleen! (I have always fancied she must have been lonely.) But if you were to meet her now, Mr. Seymour, with the changes of the past years upon her, do you think she would be 'Kathleen Mavourneen' to you still?"

"Yes," he said. "Kathleen Mavourneen forever."

"If—if—Suppose that circumstances had made her a woman of the world, a woman whose life had been full of worldly scheming, and who was called vain and heart-less—what then?"

"She could never be that," he said—"never that wholly. I am willing to trust her."

Kate had taken the lily from her hair, and was pulling it to pieces, flinging the white petals over the balcony, and watching them as they fluttered softly to the ground.

"They say truth is stranger than fiction," she said; "and I believe it is. If I were to tell you that I know something of your little Kathleen, Mr. Seymour—"

"Kate, my dear," broke in a voice from behind them, "is it fair that you should monopolize Mr. Seymour altogether? It is my impression that he called to see me; and, besides, Mr. Colycinth is waiting for you. Have you forgotten your promise to him?"

Kate turned round with a calm, unshaken composure.

"Certainly not," she said. "You will excuse me, Mr. Seymour. I promised to drive with Mr. Colycinth this evening."

Carl bowed, and turned to the aunt. He did not remain long, however. He was moved and excited as he had never been before in his life. What if, at last—at last he had found his child-love again. To some men, the boyish romance would have been merely an amusing incident, pleasant to look back upon; but to Carl Seymour it was an earnest truth, and might yet rule his whole life. As he strolled homeward, he thought of it all. He could remember now how the memory of the innocent eyes and pure lips had restrained and comforted him; how he had dreamed of the childish face that had once nestled against his breast. The soft, distant sound of the waves brought back to him the time when Kathleen had fallen asleep in his arms, and he had carried her two miles over the shore, looking down at her, and wondering if ever woman or child was so fair as this little maiden. Mark you, it was not of Kate Davenant he was dreaming—it was of Kathleen Ogilvie. The time had not yet come when he could understand that he loved the woman for what the child had been. Now and again, something rose up before him vaguely, some thought which tried to connect this woman of the world, this Circe, with his child-darling; but in some way he could not make it clear to himself, and so wandered back almost unconsciously to the old romance.

CHAPTER V.

IT MAY BE FOR YEARS.

THE last sunbeam had faded, and the twilight set in, as he reached the Ocean House. Gerald Colycinth's carriage at that moment dashed by, and Miss Davenant, in a pearly silk, and a fairy hat, waved her exquisitely gloved hand to him and smiled. He found Brandon waiting for him. Poor Fred Brandon, in the tightest of boots and the most remarkable of "get ups," and looking most abominably doleful. He, too, had been added to the Circe's train. Like Tom Griffith, he had paid ruinous prices for bouquets for Miss Davenant to laugh at.

"I've been to Bay View," he said, dismally. "Got there just in time to see that beggar, Colycinth, drive off with Miss Davenant. Confound it all!"

A month ago, Seymour would have shrugged his shoulders and drawn down the corners of his handsome mouth; but now he was silent, and—ah! far worse—felt a little curious pang for which he could not account. Brandon grumbled eloquently. First, at the heat; next, at his boots; then at his tailor; but, most of all, at "that muff of a Colycinth." At last he started up to the window, with an exclamation of surprise.

"Here's Carver coming down the avenue. Mrs. Montgomery's footman, you know. Wonder where he is going to! Jove! he's turning in here!"

The correct footman was indeed entering the hotel. Carl caught the last glimpse of his blue and drab livery as he passed up the steps.

"What can he be coming for?" said he, carelessly. Before he had finished speaking, a slim cream-colored envelope was handed to him, stamped with a scarlet monogram, and directed in a delicate hand. Carl Seymour's face was generally a calm one, and noticeable for its fine ivory pallor; but as he opened the note it changed and flushed, and his shapely hand shook a little. The note ran thus:

"DEAR MR. SEYMOUR—Of course, you have received an invitation for the Amateur Concert? If I see you there to-night, I will show you the woman the world has made of 'Kathleen Mavourneen.' KATE DAVENANT."

Brandon looked curiously at his companion, as he folded the note slowly and replaced it in its envelope. The flush had died out of his face and left it colorless, as usual, but his hand was not steady yet, and his lips were half trembling.

"Going to the concert to-night?" he asked, at last.

Brandon nodded, and replied, "That amateur affair, you mean? Yes. Alice Farnham introduced two or three tableaux into the programme, and Miss Davenant is great on tableaux."

Carl hardly heard him. He was thinking of the "woman the world had made of Kathleen Mavourneen."

His wild fancies were proving themselves true, or, at least, he could only place that construction upon the letter he held in his hand. The few intervening hours between its arrival and the concert seemed fairly to drag themselves away. When Brandon had gone, he went up to his sleeping-room,.and watched the twilight deepen and deepen upon the distant sea, until the blue had darkened into purple, and until the purple was hung with dewy-eyed stars, and the great pearl moon swung high in the dome of heaven. Now and again he turned to glance at the lily-set Clytie, gleaming whitely where the moonlight struck snowy shoulder and exquisite face. He did not quite understand the thrill, that was almost like a pain as it touched him, and he felt half-impatient at it; but still the thrill was there, and in spite of its tenderness, pain lay beneath it.

But at length the hours of waiting were over, and he was seated in the little, crowded theatre. Amateur concerts and entertainments were pretty Alice Farnham's hobby; and she was at the head of the committee who gave this entertainment for the benefit of the family of a disabled soldier. She came to Carl, this pretty Alice, when she saw him, and bending over his seat, touched him on the shoulder with her fan.

"I am so glad you are here," she said, in her pretty, enthusiastic way. "I want you to see our tableaux. Miss Davenant arranged them nearly all. Look at your programme, and you will see her name in half a dozen."

Carl looked at the scented trifle of rose-tinted paper and gold lettering, and ran over the list. He noticed one hand in all. The artistic taste, and theatrical genius displayed, struck him in every fresh title; but when he reached the bottom of the page he started.

"'Kathleen Mavourneen.' Song in costume, by Miss Davenant."

Alice did not see the start, for at that moment a gentleman came to take her behind the scenes.

"The curtain will be raised directly," she said to Carl. "I want you to tell me afterward what you think of 'Louise de Valliere.'"

Five minutes after, the curtain was drawn up. The scene was the interior of a small Gothic chapel. Saints stood in the niches, and angels folded their wings above the stained-glass windows. At one end, in the dim, mellow light, a white marble cross stood revealed, and before this cross knelt a woman. This was the chapel of the Carmelites, and the kneeling figure was Louise de Valliere. Her heavy, pall-like, velvet robe swept the tiled floor behind her; her exquisite eyes were uplifted, full of pleading passion and despair; her hands clung to a rosary, and a richly-bound missile lay beside her, bearing upon its cover the miniature of her lost lover and king. Carl remembered the star-white face and purple eyes long after that, and shuddered as he thought of their despair, and the hollow sound of the tolling convent-bell. When, at last, the curtain fell, the audience broke into a storm of well-bred applause. Every one knew the perfect face, and dark-brown, unbound hair, and Miss Davenant's list of victims swelled to countless numbers.

There seemed to be a great deal of curiosity about the final song. Carl could hear questioning comments on every side. What could be made of "Kathleen Mavourneen?" people asked. In fact, the audience were quite anxious about it. But could the most anxious be more

4

anxious than this man to whom this song was to be the
solution of a problem? He waited for it more than impatiently. Every now and then he caught sight of Miss
Davenant passing to and fro, smiling and jesting, and
listening to the repeated compliments, with the perfection
of graceful good-breeding, which was habitual to her, and
with her soft, low laugh, ringing sometimes like music.

But at length the end of the programme was reached.
Seymour was almost glad when the curtain fell upon
" King Arthur and Guinevere."

" Last, but not least," said a voice behind him. " 'Kathleen Mavourneen.' Song in costume, by Miss Davenant.
Now we may expect a *bonbon* of artistic taste."

There was a little pause, a sort of rest for five minutes,
in which the audience waited breathlessly, as an eager
audience will wait, and then the curtain rose again.

A little, broken hut, all tree-shadowed, a gray, old
lichen-covered rock, by the side of a clear, deep-looking
spring, and in the softened, stage-moonlight, a girl standing
alone. No expense had been spared to make the scenery
natural. Carl knew the picture, and knew the slight,
girlish figure resting against the old gray stone. A very
slight figure it looked now, in the short, blue skirt and
laced bodice, and more girlish than Miss Davenant had

ever seemed before. A little scarlet cloak hung round her, and her hair fell loosely from its hood. Her very face seemed changed, as the soft, subdued light fell upon it. For a moment, there was a dead, breathless silence, and then she took a hesitating step forward, and began her song. We all know it—the soft, soft music and tender words. The orchestra, like all the other arrangements, was a piece of perfection, and the low throb of the accompaniment rose like a deeper, fuller echo of every note she sung. Carl leaned forward—he could not help it—and after the first glance, shaded his face with his gloved hand, and only listened. Her little, fair hands hung clasped before her, and the voice that "fell like a falling star" upon the enraptured audience, fell full of unshed tears. Ah! who shall say but that the purest part of her life came back to her then! who shall say but that if she might only have awakened in the moonlight a child once more, the white angels might have saved her from the fever-dream of the life she had lived! Then it was, but never till then, that Carl Seymour knew all he had lost, and all he had won; then, and not till then, did it come home to him, as a truth, a passionate, living truth, that this Kate Davenant and Kathleen Ogilvie, who were one and the same, held one and the same place in his heart.

"It may be for years, and it may be forever;
    Ah! why art thou silent, thou voice of my heart!"

Then he looked up at her and met her eyes, the eyes
of child Kathleen, the eyes he had loved all these long
years.

The song was ended, and as the last note died away, the
spell upon her listeners was broken, and the applause
burst forth.

The little theatre had never heard such a tumult before.
It swelled, and rang, and echoed again with bravos, and
encores, and clappings. The select audience forgot that
it was select, and became enthusiastic, and when the fair
singer reappeared, bouquets were showered upon her.
Carl had only a waxen-cupped camelia, but as it fell at
her feet, Miss Davenant stooped and picked it up, and
held it in her hand as she repeated her song. And then
it was all over, and the crush and tumult of departure
began. Carl made his way behind the scenes, and met
Alice Farnham.

"Ah, here you are!" said the young lady. "Miss
Davenant is in the manager's room. I think she is expecting you."

"Miss Davenant!" he heard. "Miss Davenant!" on
every side among the amateurs; and then he found him-

self in the little apartment dignified by the title of the
manager's room, standing before her—"Kathleen Mavourneen," or Kate Davenant—which? Kate Davenant now,
for she had changed her stage-dress, and waited in her
graceful trailing robes.

Kate Davenant for a moment, and then she forgot herself, and looked up and down, and almost trembled; and
the great tears stood in her eyes, and she was silent as
though she could not speak. Seymour forgot himself, too.
His calm, haughty, emotionless self was lost, and he came
to her and took hold of her hands, and held them, and
looked down into her eyes, down, down, as no man had
ever looked before.

"The woman the world has made of little Kathleen,"
he said. "I thought I had lost you, mavourneen; and
you have come back to me. To me!" he said. "To
me!"

"What am I to say?" she said, with a little trembling
sweetness in her voice. "I am not Kathleen Ogilvie—I
am Kate Davenant, what the world and its worldliness
has left of your child, Kathleen."

"I am willing to trust you," was the answer. "Tell
me, who wove this web for me?"

"My aunt, as I call her," she said, with the smile again.

"But I am really her cousin, by a fiftieth remove. For the sake of the old blood, and my Davenant face, she took me, and amused herself with educating me. Davenant was my father's name, and—and—" the patrician face flushed a little as she hesitated over her speech, "the world never knew that my mother had a right to it; she was but a poor girl of Irish parentage, whom he fell in love with when he was yachting on the coast of Maine, and secretly married."

Carl had not loosened his grasp upon her hands, but just then she remembered herself and dropped them from his clasp.

"I knew you from the first," she said, smiling. "When you gave me my glove at Mrs. Farnham's croquet-party, I recollected your face, and connected it with your name, while you, faithless cavalier, had forgotten all."

"No," he answered, "I had not forgotten, but I could not believe."

Having had time to recover her composure, she was quite Miss Davenant, now. Miss Davenant softened, perhaps, but still the Circe.

"I must find my aunt," she said, her eyes a little down-cast, under his steady gaze. "Will you please take me to her?"

He laid her hand upon his arm, and held it in his own until he helped her into her carriage; then, with his farewell, he looked down at her again, as if waiting for something.

The time had come when Miss Davenant had found a controlling power, and her eyelids drooped.

"Come to-morrow," she said, timidly. "I want—I should like to talk to you about old times."

Carl smiled, as she had not seen him smile before; a smile that brought the blood into her cheeks.

"I have found you," he said. "I will not lose you again."

Then the carriage drove off.

"Kate," said Mrs. Montgomery, "that man is not going to make a second Tom Griffith of himself; and you ought to know better than to meddle with edge-tools, unless you wish to cut your fingers."

Carl went home to his hotel, and found a moon-beam resting upon the Clytie's face.

"The woman the world has made of Kate Ogilvie," he whispered. "I loved you then, I love you now. I will trust you, if I risk my life upon it—darling!"

He bent over and kissed the cold, white shoulder with his passionate lips.

CHAPTER VI.

BY THE SAD SEA.

THE next morning, Miss Davenant's maid brought her a new style of floral-offering. It was a fragile basket, lined with moss-like, emerald velvet, and full of cool, dewy-looking lilies, with great, golden eyes and waxen leaves, and in their centre glowed a blood-red camelia. Kate was dressing lazily when it came, and she only told Lotte to leave it on the flower stand, without making any comment.

But when the girl left the room, the cheeks, scarcely tinted before, looked like the camelia-petals, and a curious, regretful glow burned in her eyes as she took the artistic trifle in her hand.

"I wonder if I am a very wicked woman?" she said. "Perhaps I had better have remained nothing but Miss Davenant to him. If there had never been a Kathleen Ogilvie, my life might have been smoother, or, at least, more bearable. But I can't look back, and then be content to look forward."

I wonder if you have found out by this time that there

was a good and a bad angel in Kate Davenant's life, and
that the time had come now when either one or the other
must rule forever. Imagine a girl, with every beauty
and fascination, given into the hands of such a woman as
Mrs. Mortimer Montgomery; a woman who had lived in
the world, and for the world, since she escaped from the
nursery ; who had paused to think of nothing but the
luxurious gayety her refinement and wealth were so well
able to procure her. If it had not been for the patrician,
Davenant face, Kathleen Ogilvie might have remained
Kathleen Ogilvie; but there was a pleasant *eclat* in playing the part of chaperon to a girl who was likely to carry
the world before her. Beyond that she thought of nothing. Kate might be educated, and introduced to society,
and then she might marry—*un bon parti*, of course. No
other idea had ever occurred to the selfish aunt. Kate
had lived a life that would unfit her for any other. Kate
had seen belles and beauties making love-matches, and
finally sinking into domestic insignificance, mending
stockings, sewing on buttons, and adding up the house-
keeping accounts. "Seen," I said. I ought to have said,
"heard of," for these sort of people fell from Mrs. Montgomery's circle and lapsed into nothingness. Kate had
heard these same nonentities discussed, and seen them

snubbed, and observed the resigned, tolerant shrug with
which society greeted them when they came within range
of respectability's eye-glass. "Respectability (which,
when it did not signify millionaires, signified billionaires,
or trillionaires) was very sorry for the girl. It was a
great pity. But what could be expected after such an
insane match as that;" and then Respectability shrugged
its shoulders again and forgot to recognize the fallen star.
Kate had lived among women whose lives were one long
struggle to out-do each other in magnificence, and who kept
a troupe of French nursemaids in a well-appointed nursery,
and "forgot to ask about baby," and called in to see the
children twice a week. What do you suppose such an
experience could make of such a girl as this heroine of
mine? It made of her just such a woman as the rest, just
as coolly refined and calculating, only with a little more
brains, and a little sting of remorseful longing for something unattainably better, which sometimes made her life
wearisome and galling. Her future was laid before her,
a future which her training compelled her to accept, and
which was a sort of game in which her white hands moved
the pieces. Still, if she must marry a millionaire, this
was no reason, she argued, why she should not amuse
herself with men, who were amusing in spite of their

empty pockets. There was an excitement in the whirl
that made her a belle and almost a goddess. There was
an excitement in the bowing of the *creme de la creme* of
penniless Bohemians. When she drove in her carriage
through crowded thoroughfares, rough workmen and
elegant men turned round alike to gaze after her, and
comment upon her flawless beauty; and once, when she
had attended a court-ball in Paris, the emperor himself
had spoken flatteringly of her. Since her sixteenth year
she had been " *la belle Circe*," " *Sylphide*," " *Superbe;* "
and now, at nineteen, she laughed at the men who raved
about her, and wrote poems in her honor, laughed at
them, yet held them in the palm of her delicate, careless
hand still. It was only the " Marquise " again.

> " You were belle *cruelle, rebelle,*
> And the rest of rhymes as well.
> You had every grace in Heavèn
> In your most angelic face,
> With the nameless finer leaven,
> Lent of blood and courtly race;
> And was added, too, in duty,
> Ninon's wit and Bouffler's beauty,
> And La Valliere's " *yeux caloutes* "
>   Followed these;
> And you liked it when he said it,
>   On his knees,
> And you kept it, and you read it,
>   Belle Marquise."

Just this it was that made the girl color as she looked
at the flower-offering. She could understand its meaning,
and knew what it would end in. And then—and then
(woman of the world as she was, she hesitated a little as
the thought came to her) might it not end in some faint
pang to herself? There had been times in her life before
now when the world had seemed a thought darker after
handsome, manly faces had turned away from her, paling
in despair, yet showing something of scorn for the fallen
idol. But Carl Seymour was different from even the best
of these. The man's very soul was strong, and his power
over men, women, and children, was his chief characteristic.
She had heard his acquaintance talking of him and wondering at his perfect fascination.

"He's such a cool, immobile sort of a fellow!" Tom
Griffith had said, one day. "But every man he speaks
to respects and looks up to him. By George! the very
horses in the stable whine and turn their big, velvet eyes
when he lays his hand upon them."

Was not this a trifle dangerous?

Kate leaned her firm, white chin upon her palm, and
her purple eyes widened and darkened under their fringes
as she thought it over. Why was it that this bondage was
her fate? Why was it that the whole sum of her existence
lay in the one channel?

"If I were only Kate Ogilvie now!" she exclaimed, almost involuntarily, with her scarlet lips parted wistfully. "If he had only found me little Kate again, innocent and good in spite of all! I might—I might—"

She stopped, and the warm color rushed over her face. She was treading on forbidden ground. She laid the basket upon the table, and rang the bell for Lotte.

"You may dress my hair now, Lotte," she said; "and fasten that red camelia in the puffs with a spray of white coral."

Lotte pulled it all down, the dark-brown, burnished hair, with its heavy braids and soft curves, and began to dress it in discreet silence; and under the gold-dusted mantle the Circe bent her head and watched the marble-cupped lilies, and tried to think she was a girl again, and Carl Seymour had the right to call her "Kathleen Mavourneen."

That evening Mr. Colycinth drove his carriage over the beach alone, for when he had called at Bay View he found the Circe "not at home."

"Gone to the Spouting Horn with Mr. Seymour," said her aunt, with some dissatisfaction apparent in her manner. "Kate has a craze about scenery. Just imagine any one walking a mile over the sands for the sake of getting a good view of sky and water!"

This was anything but satisfactory to the "literary lion." Miss Davenant seldom, if ever, promenaded with her adorers. Was not this a foreboding state of affairs, when she walked a mile with a happy hero?

And in the meantime the Circe forgot herself, strolling over the shining sands, with the shining sea before her, and the shining sky above. The purple water dimpled and whispered, and the evening breeze swept a soft pink into her waxen cheek, and a soft light came into her eyes. She felt like Kate Ogilvie again, and once or twice a tender, womanly thrill crept over her, as she looked up at her companion's earnest face. For Carl Seymour he failed to remember that it was a worldly-wise woman he was talking to, and not an innocent, inexperienced girl. Yellow sands, and sunset sky, and lapping waves, seemed so familiar that he thought only of the years behind, and the child who had lived in them. When they reached the cliffs at last, they found they were the only visitors. Carl leaned against a jutting fragment and looked down at Miss Davenant's fair face.

"Why did you not tell me at first?" he asked, going on with the conversation.

Kate colored a little.

"It was an impulse that made me tell you at all," she

said. "An impulse, and the fact that you had almost found me out."

"But that is not replying to my question. Why was this?"

A wish, almost uncontrollable, came up into the girl's mind—a wish that was the result of the truth that really lay buried in her heart. If she could only make him understand her position, if he could but just see how utterly impossible it was for the woman to be to him what the child had been. There was a sharp struggle, and then she made a brave trial—a trial that needed a struggle in spite of all.

"Do you recollect what I said to you yesterday afternoon on the balcony, and what I repeated in the manager's room? Nine years ago I was a child, Mr. Seymour. Now I am a woman, and because I wish to be more frank with you than I am to others, I will tell you again that I am afraid Kate Davenant is very unlike the child you loved so well."

Carl looked down at her flushing face, with a curious awakening in his eyes, but he did not speak.

"Do you know what the world says of me, Mr. Seymour?" she went on. "The world says I am a vain, heartless woman, caring for nothing but my own triumphs.

Perhaps the world is right, though it may be somewhat harsh. Still, you know a girlhood spent as mine has been, cannot make one very unworldly and single-hearted."

She had looked very unlike the Circe when she began to speak, but she looked wonderfully unlike her when, coming to the end of the last sentence, she broke forth again, with the hot color flushing her cheeks, and her eyes full of vague bitterness.

"I am saying to you what I have said to no man or woman before. I say it, because as you cared for the lonely little Kathleen, so you may, perhaps, feel an interest in this other Kate, who is lonelier now than ever she was then. Shall I tell you why my aunt took me up? She took me because I had a pretty face; she took me because I was a bright, amusing child, and my beauty was likely to make a belle of me. She took me because she thought I was a good speculation, just as her lions and lionesses are, and she made of me what you see—a beauty, people tell us, and an elegant, worldly-wise belle, according to society's report—Kate Davenant, in short, and not the best woman you know, by any means."

I repeat the conversation, reader, to prove to you that this girl was not wholly heartless; to show you, for her credit, that she made one effort, if only one, to save this man, and that it was hardly her fault if this effort failed. I also wish you to remember, when you read the history of its failure, that for ten years Carl Seymour had loved her, however unconsciously; that she had held the place in his heart that a woman will sometimes hold in the heart and life of a man like him—in the heart of a man hard to rule, but conquered utterly and wholly, when at last he meets a ruling power.

He bent over her, and took both her slender gloved hands in a grasp that was almost painful.

"You ask me to remember what you have told me," he said with glowing eyes. "Remember what I have said to you, 'Kathleen Mavourneen will be Kathleen Mavourneen forever!' So you are to me."

Then her resolution broke down. She had made such an effort as she was capable of, and it had failed. Perhaps, as she smiled up into Carl Seymour's passionate face, her good angel folded its white wings and wept. She had not learned to be strong in truth, and after this first struggle, she gave herself up, as she had given herself up before, to the current which carried her onward to another's undoing.

When they returned to Bay View, they found a gay company gathered there. Mrs. Montgomery's eyebrows were uplifted a little, as the two sauntered in, the Circe's eyes uplifted softly to her companion.

Tom Griffith looked at Brandon and collapsed. The senator became majesterially grave, and one or two of the "fast" men began to comment.

"This is a new one, ain't it? How new? About six weeks old. Poor fellow!"

Carl remained for the evening. Kate chattered and laughed with all. But Carl did not understand, nay, it was impossible for him to understand the truth—that the gayety and carelessness had a touch of desperation in it. He did not dream of the vague, passionate aching that lay behind the brilliant repartee and laughter; and the curious, almost mad emphasis that urged Kate Davenant to jest and merriment, when the heart that seemed to beat so calmly beneath her trim bodice was stung with blind regret. Once, when he spoke to her in a sort of forgetfulness, called her by the old name, "Kathleen," when he had said it, he stopped, and smiled at his carelessness.

"Forgive me," he said. "I forgot there are nine years behind us. Am I very impertinent?"

"No," she replied, impulsively. "I like to hear it. I wish you would call me Kathleen always. It is like oil upon troubled waters," she added, with a laugh that was almost bitter in its recklessness.

Hitherto Miss Davenant's flirtations had rejoiced in one peculiarity; their advance had been almost imperceptible, and one victim had hardly seemed more honored than another. But this evening the rule was broken, and Mr. Seymour's position attracted comment. The purple eyes seemed to turn to him as if unavoidably, the sweet face to answer his every expression. Alice Farnham had Tom Griffith all to herself, and Brandon was left to mourn alone, while the senator, the poor senator, and the rest of the train, could only stand aloof with a united expression of stolid misery and resigned despair.

When the company separated, and Carl had spoken his last "Kathleen," Miss Davenant did not wait to hear her aunt's eloquence on her dangerous proclivities, but went up-stairs to her room.

"Please send me some strong coffee, aunt," she said. "I have a headache."

"You will kill yourself with strong coffee, Kate. It is a sort of intoxication with you." Whereupon Kate shrugged her shoulders indifferently, and smiled.

After the strong coffee, there were notes to be read, and replies to make—and Kate set to work upon them with uncalled-for energy; and when they were done, she undressed and tried to sleep. But sleep would not come.

The murmur of the distant sea came up to her moaningly, and made her restless; and her thoughts kept her feverishly wide awake. At last she sprung up, threw on a wrapper, and going to the window, looked out. The deserted grounds lay below, breathing up the perfume of the sleeping flowers, and whispering under the night-wind softly. Through the dark trees came a silvery shimmer of moonlight. She watched it all in a dreamy silence for a while, and then suddenly turned away, and coming to the dressing-table, opened a little jewel-case, and took out a chain of sea-shells, and a chain of gold, and laid them by the side of the red camelia. It was a curious thing she was going to do, and might seem whimsical but a great deal depended upon it.

"I will try once more," she said to herself. "Once more, and for the last time. If Fate guides my hand to the gold—so be it."

She retreated a few steps backward, then turned round with closed eyes, and stood still. She was smiling lightly, and, perhaps, a little satirically, but her heart was beating, nevertheless, with a fierce pained heat. Did she then care so much? A half struggle, a step forward, her white hands fluttered over the curious omens of her future, and then descending, touched—what? She turned her face again paling and blushing. The spirit of flower and shells melted away, and a slight shiver passed over her. She had touched the gold.

She laughed a short, strange, impatient laugh as she crushed shells and chain back into the case.

"There were two chances against one," she whispered, sharply. "I suppose it is fate!"

CHAPTER VII.

WAVERING.

"WHAT do you think of it?" asked Brandon, doubtfully.

Captain Loftus, who was this young man's oracle, and was obliging enough to borrow his money and smoke his cigars, held a glass of fine old Madeira to the light and criticised its color with the air of a connoisseur.

"How old are you, my boy?" he asked.

Brandon stared.

"Twenty-two," he said, with a little extra color on his honest fair face.

"Thought so," moralized the captain. "At twenty-two I was guileless—it is a long time back, though—but I got over that in the course of time, as you will. Now, I understand arithmetic, and experience teaches me that, in sensible people's eyes, Seymour's talent and far-off fortune won't stand in exchange and barter against the Circe. You have seen rare paintings in collections of art wearing the green ticket, haven't you? I am not good at comparisons generally, but I never see such pictures without thinking of some of our belles. Kate Davenant was one of them, and her owner (see her aunt) has marked her at a higher price than Seymour can afford to give for years to come; and in years to come the gilt would be worn off the frame, and the picture might not be considered worth the prize. *Comprenez vous, mon enfant ?* "

The captain laughed.

"A sentiment of two decades again. If Miss Davenant had been the susceptible Miss Brown, or the adorable Miss Smith, the tender passion might be a ruling consideration; but Miss Davenant is a wise woman—a woman of *our* world, which is not the world of Brown, Jones and Robinson. Picture the Circe anxious about the rise of mutton and interested in the fall of beef. Imagine the woman, whom report says royalty has pronounced '*charmante,*' with Vanity Fair in the background, and domestic felicity in Blank street for a future. What a fall would be there! Oh! my youthful countryman! Miss Davenant knows better."

"Well, then," exclaimed Brandon, reddening to the very roots of his blond hair, "it's—it's a confounded shame she should lead him on so. I've been as spoony as any one myself, but I am not such a deep fellow as Seymour, and I know I felt bad enough about it—and what will it be to him? Every one knows he loves the very

dead leaves her feet have trodden upon. It has changed
him altogether. Every picture he paints has some tint or
expression that belongs to her. People say that 'Louise
la Valliere,' with her face, is a master-piece; and there is
one he calls 'Kathleen Mavourneen' (taken from that
scene she acted in at the amateur concert), has got something in it that I'm afraid to look at. By Jove! it makes
me tremble. His very soul is laid bare in it."

Loftus laughed a short, recklessly sounding laugh.

"You haven't seen that sort of thing before?" he said.
"I have. Women don't stand at broken hearts in these
days. A girl of the Davenant pattern made me what I
am. Forty thousand a year bought her. I couldn't. If
I could, I might have been a respectable *pater-familias*
now, with some pretty little girls of my own to take care
of and try to save from being put up at auction. Well,
well! three-score-and-ten is the end of it all—and we live
fast in this generation. But I am sorry for you, my boy.
How did you manage to have your eyes opened?"

"It wasn't anything of a joke to me, I can tell you," was
the half-sheepish reply. "I knew I had no chance against
Seymour, but I told her the truth, one night, because I
couldn't help it. I think she was sorry for me. She said
she was, and that I must forget it and try to love a better
woman."

"Tender-hearted creature!" sneered Loftus. "How terribly she must have suffered! I wonder how many other fools—excuse me— have received like consolation."

"Don't speak like that," broke out poor Brandon. "I know I'm a fool, but I haven't quite outlived it yet; and I can't let any one sneer at her. My mother says" (the good-natured youngster hadn't outlived his mother yet) "that good mothers make good daughters. Kate Davenant's mother died when she was born."

Loftus forgot to sneer again. Something of the heart that was seared twenty years back stirred in him as he laid his hand on the young man's shoulder.

"You are a good-hearted fellow," he said, with a new warmth on his face. "And you ought to love a better woman than Kate Davenant. Try to get over it, and let me tell you one thing. Try to keep your heart fresh, and don't live so that the time will come when you look back and shudder, and look forward and see only six feet of earth and nothingness. That is what my youth has led me to."

What Brandon had said was true. Because he had loved no other woman, Carl Seymour loved this Kate as none had loved her before. A calm, haughty-spirited man forgets himself entirely when he meets his destiny. Kate Dave-

nant was his destiny.   Every picture he touched wore some
unconsciously inwrought charm that belonged to her.   One,
her heavy, dark brown hair, with its metallic sheen and
sparks of fiery gold; another, her red, red lips; another, the
dark, loving purple of her eyes, and the exquisite, touching
smile.   She had become an inspiration to him, and the
Clytie on the mantel had grown to his very soul.   Here
she knelt in the dim cloister of the Carmelite convent as
"la Valliere," there she stood erect in her war-chariot as
grand-eyed Boadicea, with crowds of shaggy-haired, wild-
faced Icenians gazing upon her with fierce, hungry eyes.
People recognized the Guinevere, who knelt at Arthur's
feet, her coiling tresses trailing over her outstretched arms
upon the marble floor, and the " Court Lady," who held
the cross before the dying soldier, won its hundreds
because the man who bought it loved the eyes that lived
upon it.

Mrs. Montgomery had become dissatisfied, and Carl
had learned to understand that a little indescribable coldness lay between himself and his former admirer.   Kate
let herself drift on wherever the current carried her.   She
had grown hardened and careless to the pain and happiness that grew upon her day by day.   She knew where it
must all end, and only tried to delay what must come at

last. Sometimes her bitterness struggled above all, and leaped out; and sometimes the delicious draught she was drinking, for the first time in her life, was so sweet, so maddeningly sweet, that the bitterness was overruled, and she shut her heart to every remembrance of the unwomanly wrong she was doing.

She came in upon her aunt one day with some fairy-web sea-weed in her hand. Her eyes were drooping, and her lips curved softly in a curious, dreamy, absent-mindedness. There was a little boat down in the bay that bore her name, and for the last hour she had held the tiller and steered to Carl Seymour's rowing, as they floated in the golden mist that rested upon the waters. There was sea and sky before, and the purple rocks and the world behind. And in the lapses of dreaming thought that came upon her, Kate had wished that they might drift onward forever, and lose themselves in the crimson and gold beyond. When she entered the parlor, she was thinking of his face as he had looked at her in silence. Just what a man's face will say sometimes to a woman, his face had said to her, and, perhaps, hers had answered him a little. She loved him. She had not hidden that from herself from the first; and once or twice it was too much for her, and the whole truth shimmered in the soft rose on her cheek, and the drooping of the heavily-fringed white lids. He had not spoken, he had only rested upon his oars, and let the boat drift, as he watched her averted face ; and she could not forget—she thought she never could forget—the faint, passionate trembling of the mouth that was usually so calm.

Mrs. Montgomery looked up, as she came in, with a cold inquiry in her manner.

"Where have you been?" she asked.

"Sailing with Mr. Seymour," answered Kate, indifferently, as she drew off her gloves.

There was a silence for a few moments, in which she laid the sea-weed among the rest of her collection. As she turned to leave the room her aunt spoke again.

"When you have changed your dress, I wish you would come down-stairs again. I want to speak to you."

Kate turned back with a calm smile.

"I can stay just as well now," she said. "What is it you wish to say?"

Her aunt stitched at her embroidery energetically, and then she looked up.

"Kate," she said, "I am going to say what I have said a thousand times before. You are going too far."

Kate's eyebrows were uplifted nonchalantly, but she made no reply.

"In this case," proceeded the lady, "you are going too far for your own comfort. You are not sentimentally inclined by any means; but you know as well as I do that this man is more to you than any other has ever been. I don't wonder at it, either. He is a man a great deal above his position, and, of course, it is a pity; but still you ought to be wise enough to know better than allow yourself to think of him seriously. Flowers, and poems, and pictures, are all very well; but a man can't use his eyes and his brains, as this man is doing, without making some impression. He kissed your hand last night. I saw him. And when you were waltzing together, you could no more have lifted your eyes to his face than you could have done anything else impossible. You know what your position is, and you know—well, you know that this sort of thing won't do."

It would be a hard matter to try to describe the various expressions that passed over Kate Davenant's countenance as she listened First, it was haughty defiance, then bitter, bitter scornfulness, and at last coldness, perfectly immobile.

"Yes," she said, "I know that this 'sort of thing won't do.' I know my position as well as you know it, and understand it as thoroughly. I know what my life has fitted me for, and I know that I must prepare myself for the future lying before me. We have talked of this before, I believe, and it has always ended in the same thing. Thank you for reminding me of my danger; but, as you say, I am not a sentimental woman by any means, and I am not likely to swerve on the side of romantic weakness. Excuse my being a trifle bitter. Probably I *was* forgetting, and allowing myself to dream such dreams as only better and richer women may indulge in."

Her aunt shrugged her shoulders resignedly.

"I didn't think it was so bad as this," she said, satirically. "I must say you *are* a trifle bitter. Of course, it is no affair of mine. Perhaps, on the whole, you had better marry Mr. Seymour, if you can make up your mind to conversations with the butcher, and eloquence from the baker. In the course of ten years, I dare say, he will be a celebrated artist, and in the meantime, you know, you could retire from society, and superintend your two servants, and have your dresses made by a third-rate *modiste.* You would not miss your acquaintance after a while, and it is not so very dreadful to be snubbed; and then, you know, what are these trifling sacrifices to domestic felicity?"

"Is that all you wished to say?" asked Kate, after the

minute's silence that followed her ladyship's harangue. "If it is, I think I will go up-stairs now. You know we dine at the Farnhams, and I should like to rest before dressing."

"Well, it isn't quite all," was the reply. "I wanted to tell you that Mr. Crozier called this evening and inquired about you particularly. I said he would meet us at Mrs. Farnham's to-night."

Kate paled slightly.

"I did not know he had come to Newport," she said.

"He arrived yesterday. Kate, how foolish you were to refuse that man! He is worth two millions."

"Was I?" said Kate. "If Mr. Crozier had been worth fifty millions instead of two, you would have said I was very wise. But, perhaps, it is not too late yet," and she laughed a short, reckless laugh, that was a little terrible.

Her aunt did not say anything. She knew her fair niece well enough to understand that it was best not to interfere with her in these moods.

Kate went to her room in a curious frame of mind, and sat down and looked matters in the face. That she loved Carl Seymour she knew, but her love was not like his, it could not reconcile her to all things for his sake. Her experience had not been calculated to make her understand that the time would come when sacrifice would be as nothing. A blind instinct gave her the tender, womanly thoughts that thrilled her, but the motives that had ruled her life held her back with a cold hand. She was bitter and restive under her bondage, but she could not break it. She had laughed at sentiment since her girlhood, and for nine years had thought of nothing but the one ending to her belledom, for which her far-seeing relative had educated her. But wise as she was, Mrs. Montgomery had not foreseen this. She had felt no qualms of conscience and galling regret, there had been no struggle for mastery between heart and head in her days, and so she only regarded Kate's impulses of rebellion as symptoms of "blues," and accordingly had felt no concern.

It did not occur to her that the ten innocently-childish years could not fail to leave their traces behind. Those ten years had left traces.

CHAPTER VIII.

WHO WINS—PAYS.

BEFORE Kate had been seated for five minutes, she sprung up from her chair and paced the floor backward and forward, trying to forget herself. Her aunt's sarcasm had been a bitter truth to her, and she felt that she had almost reached the end of her tether. What had she done? Nothing wrong, she tried to think—nothing more than she had done a hundred times before, only before no suffering had been entailed upon herself. Now she must suffer, as she had made others suffer; now her dainty feet must tread the same thorny path other feet had trod for her sake. Perhaps her aunt had been right in saying she was foolish in refusing Mr. Crozier, when, two years ago, he had offered her marriage. If she had married him then, by this time she would have learned to wear her fetters gracefully, and certainly she would have been spared this pain. Her aunt's maxim on love was a concise and striking one, and one which always acted as her text.

"It is all very pretty to talk about, my dear," she had said

6

a thousand times to her niece. "But whatever motive you may marry from, you will find, in the end, that I speak truly. Years will warm the coldest love to friendship, and cool the warmest to the same sentiment." And Kate at last believed it. For three months she had floated with the current in a sort of blindly determined resistlessness, and now she must put forth her strength and battle against it. Very well.

She walked across the floor slowly, listening with a curiously acute sensation to the soft rustle of her trailing dress, and endeavoring to fix her mind calmly.

But it was a vain endeavor. There was no calmness, nothing but chaos, and a sting of self-contempt that rose above all. Every moment it grew stronger. When a woman reaches self-contempt she has reached the acme of bitterness. Kate Davenant did not pause to think, she would not pause. She loved this man, and yet was not true enough to brave sacrifice for him. · She hated herself for it, felt a vague scorn through every fibre, and yet had no other thought but that she was powerless against herself. What do you think of her? You think that Carl Seymour might have better loved a truer woman, and that if he lost her, his loss was hardly great. Yes; but then think of the "might have been;" think of the beautiful possibilities of truthfulness and faith that had been crushed out of her life. Try to imagine what she would have been, untrammeled by the world. We don't blame a flower for what the soil and the gardener's training have made it. Such women as these need praying for; and when you meet such a one give her your prayers, because you are a woman yourself, and so should be tender and forgiving.

A rap at the door stopped Kate's restless walk, and Lotte entered with a note and two bouquets. One was of fragrant lemon-blossom, white bell syringæ, and trailing with delicate vines; the other, a gorgeous tropical blooming of rare exotics, glowing with winy-crimson, purple, amber, and dark, glossy green. She knew where the first came from before she glanced at the card that accompanied it. Mr. Seymour was not a demonstrative man, and his gifts were unlike the gifts of others, in the peculiarity of being accompanied only by a slim card bearing his name.

Miss Davenant had quite a collection of them, and, in accordance with some whim, kept them apart from the notes of the slain, locking them in her jewel-case.

"With the rest of my gems," as she said, laughingly, to Carl on one occasion.

"Who brought the other?" she asked Lotte.

Lotte did not know. It was a strange footman; but here was the note.

Kate opened it with a half-amused and slightly contemptuous smile. She knew the crest which Mr. Crozier never lost an ˙opportunity of displaying; and she knew the handwriting, whose flourishes never failed to suggest business, like blue bills and legal parchment.

Mr. Crozier was a banker; Mr. Crozier had some sort of rumored interest in the East Indies. Mr. Crozier was a millionaire, if not a billionaire—some people even said a trillionaire. Twenty years ago, when Mr. Crozier was a clerk at Cent Per Cent & Co.'s, Mrs. Montgomery had been in the habit of looking upon him with something of the feeling with which one might regard a minute insect; but now—ah, now! Mr. Crozier was a sort of modern Midas, only in a more comfortable way. Oh, ye sons of man!

"John Crozier," the note was signed; and even the curly tails of the capital letters held a suggestion of unlimited wealth, giving one a very pleasant sensation of the ease with which John Crozier could sign a check. It made Miss Davenant smile. Once upon a time, the housekeeper had shown her a butcher's account, and she recollected as an amusing coincidence that Ephraim Brisket's style of caligraphy was not unlike her adorer's. But then Ephraim Brisket was not a billionaire.

"You have no need to go down-stairs again," said the young lady to Lotte. "I am ready to be dressed now."

Lotte went about her work briskly. She was a merry little maiden, with languishing eyes and scarlet lips, and tasty as a fairy, understanding how to manage to advantage every changing tint of Miss Davenant's delicate face. Kate always gave herself into Lotte's hands, with a careless confidence that each costume she turned out would be more exquisite than the last.

When she had finished dressing mademoiselle's heavy braids, she bent over to the white bouquet, and drew from it a spray of waxen japonicas and a pale-green vine. Then Miss Davenant lifted her hand and quietly pushed them aside. Lotte was only a lady's maid, and could not understand why Mr. Seymour's flowers should be rejected to-night. Miss Davenant had worn them all the summer, and had smiled and blushed at the quick-witted girl's tact. Now she did not blush. Lotte almost fancied she grew a shade paler as she pushed them aside.

"Not those, this evening," she said, quietly. "I am going to wear your favorite black lace, and you know

scarlet is the most becoming accompaniment.   Take something from the other bouquet."

Lotte's languishing eyes opened very wide, but she
said nothing.   It was not usual for Miss Davenant to
interfere with her tastes.   She must have quarrelled with
the fair-faced monsieur with the divine moustache.   Alas!

When Kate made her appearance in the parlor, her
aunt experienced a sensation of relief.   Kate had evidently
recovered from her "blues," and was going to be sensible.
The rich black lace swept in a yard of train upon the
carpet, and the thorough-bred throat and shoulders, and
superb arms, gleamed through it whitely, like bits of perfect statuary.   Her face was nothing but dazzling white
and vivid carnation, and the scarlet cardinal flowers in
the rich brown braids flung out every delicate tint artist-
ically.

Mrs. Montgomery made no remark.   She knew better,
and, besides, she recognized the flowers, and was satisfied
that her sarcasms had struck home.

When they entered Mrs. Farnham's drawing-room, the
Circe created a sensation, as she always did.   Some poetical
adorer had said of her that she was a tropical blossom,
constantly unfolding new leaves, each petal more beautiful
than the last.   So it was that people, who had seen her

before, were anxious to see her again; and those who had
never seen her were anxious to behold the woman of
whom rumor said so much. Only a few moments, and
the celebrities began to form a little cluster round her.
Fred Brandon was not there; but Tom Griffith was, looking pale and cadaverous as any modern Hamlet; and then
there were a thousand and one others, who stopped in
their passage across the room to catch a tone of the sweet
voice, or a gleam of the exquisite smile.

Her eyes wandered over the assembly in a languid
search for somebody. Carl seldom joined the train, and
somehow she had learned to watch for his coming, as she
never watched for any one else. At last, when the eyes
found him, the soft, regular heart-beat quickened a little.
He was leaning against the marble mantel, looking at her
with the old calm, searching in his face. He had looked
at her a thousand times before with just the same thought;
but now she could not meet his gaze fearlessly, and her
eyelids drooped.

She wondered if he had noticed the flowers in her hair,
and if he had noticed them, how he had accounted for
them. She felt as if their crimson burnt her cheek; and
when one of the glowing leaves touched her she positively shivered. Yet, in the meantime, she fluttered her

rose-leaf of a fan, and lifted her soft, serene eyes to Tom Griffith's face, and smiled him into a seventh heaven of delight.

"The 'Grand Mogul' has come back, Miss Davenant," said this young gentleman at last. (The "Grand Mogul" signified Mr. Crozier.)

She shrugged her white shoulders and laughed. The "Grand Mogul" was a sort of lion, as regarded bullion, and everybody knew him. Society discussed his millions and courted him. Years before, society would have pronounced him a Herculean snob, but now society knew better, and received him as a respectable fact, without making any inquiries.

"It is fortunate to be the Grand Mogul," said Kate. "But where is he, Mr. Griffith? I understood we were to meet him this evening."

Mr. Griffith did not know. He had not seen him as yet. And then he stopped short, and looked down at the fair face as if a new thought had struck him. People had a habit of speculating upon Miss Davenant, and poor Tom, who was more in love than the rest, speculated with more interest. Rumor said that John Crozier, Esq., was looking out for a wife; and rumor also said that it would not be John Crozier, Esq.'s, fault if, eventually, his home

Cul not find a mistress in Mrs. Montgomery's beautiful niece. Now Tom Griffith believed in this Kate as implicitly as if she had been an innocent *debutante*. If, at last, she married John Crozier, he would be quite content to anathematize her aunt as the root of the wrong, and regard the Circe as a heart-broken sacrifice. So now, as he noted the feverish sparkle in the girl's eyes, and the impatient ring in her voice, he felt something like pity for her, and showed it in his handsome, honest face. I wonder if you will understand me when I tell you that Kate Davenant felt a sort of anxiety about the absence of her quondam lover? She did not quite understand the feeling herself, and only accounted for it as being a wish that the first meeting was over.

But at last Mrs. Montgomery appeared, keen-eyed and stately, and a faint color showed itself on Kate's cheeks, as she recognized the gentleman her ladyship piloted with such evident satisfaction. He was a tall, burly man; so tall and burly, indeed, that he could not fail to attract attention. Neither particularly handsome, nor particularly unprepossessing, but with the bull-dog, business-like looking face which is peculiar to men of the same class.

"Ah! here she is!" said Mrs. Montgomery, catching sight of her niece. "Kate, my dear, here is Mr. Crozier."

There was nothing of the heart-broken sacrifice in Miss Davenant's manner, as she greeted the gentleman with the old, soft smile and graceful air. To tell the truth, she was so perfectly the Circe that Tom was not a little astonished. Mrs. Montgomery had been talking to Mr. Crozier, and like a wise matron had given him some little encouragement, which he would not have been likely to receive from Kate, so he felt pretty well at ease. He was not a sentimental man, and besides, he could afford to be off-hand and indifferent. He had proposed to Kate two years ago, because he wanted an aristocratic, handsome wife—and she was the handsomest and most aristocratic he could find. He had made his money, and like the generality of men like him, who have done the same thing on the same principle, had a due sense of its power and importance. If he could not marry Kate Davenant he could marry somebody else; but still he would rather have Kate Davenant. There would be more *eclat* and triumph about such a conquest. Kate knew this as well as other girls like herself knew it, and knew also that she who wore the billions must win them; and so, as Mr. Crozier seated himself at her side, she turned her aristocratic face toward him, and smiled just as she had smiled at Carl Seymour before.

"Well," said Alice Farnham, in the course of her chatter to Carl, "if Mrs. Montgomery hasn't taken that abominable Mr. Crozier to bore Kate. They do say he wanted to marry her, though I don't know how true the report is. I wonder if she would accept him? I know those flowers she is wearing came from him. Mamma's maid told me so."

Carl smiled as he looked across the room; but the next moment the smile died away. He had not noticed the flowers before, and as he caught sight of them an unaccountable chill struck him. She had worn his flowers heretofore, and now the red petals drooped and kissed her white throat as she bent forward, her eyes a little downcast, talking to the millionaire. I have said before that Seymour was not a demonstrative man, nevertheless he bit his lip fiercely as he turned to Miss Farnham again.

"Mr. Crozier is considered a good match," the young lady went on, complacently. "And somebody told me that Miss Davenant—"

But just then the stir and bustle drowned the rest of her sentence. The company were proceeding to dinner, and Carl saw Mr. Crozier rise, bowing, and then Miss Davenant's hand was slipped into his burly arm, and they passed out of the room together.

"How much would you give for Seymour's chance now?" said Brandon, to the Loftus oracle. The captain had been fastening his glove, and the button had burst from the kid and come off in his hand. He looked across the room at Carl Seymour, and then at the last sweep of the Circe's lace train.

"Look here!" he said, giving the broken fastening a cool toss into the air. "I would not risk that upon it." And the button fell upon the carpet and rolled away.

CHAPTER IX.

REALITIES.

A MONTH after this, and the autumn was paling toward winter. There were people at Newport still, but it was not so gay as before. It was too cold for picnics, and often too windy for safe sailing, and the visitors who lingered behind were preparing to leave for New York, or Boston, or Philadelphia. Some people there were who were glad the summer was over, and some looked back upon it as a pleasant remembrance. "Mrs. Grundy" had derived a great deal of amusement from the observation taken in four months. There had been plenty of room for that criticism in which "Mrs. Grundy" delighted. There had been "fast" men, and "fast" young ladies, who caused the respectable, figurative matron much righteous indignation; and, above all, there had been—Miss Davenant.

"The way that young person acted," moralized "Mrs. Grundy," "was almost disgraceful. The way the men used to rave about her, and the ridiculous poetry and nonsense they used to write was absurd. And then think how she treated that artist, you know."

This was what "Mrs. Grundy" said, and many people agreed with her. Society had always been apt to criticise Miss Davenant, but during the last two months of her stay at Newport, discussion had been very busy. Not that it was an easy matter to criticise the young lady. On the contrary, she carried her fair face and statuesque head calmly aloft throughout everything. But still there was a great deal to be said. John Crozier, Esq., had sent to Paris and brought out a miniature phaeton, and a couple of cream-colored ponies hardly bigger than rats, and on the strength of his position as *fiance* (so said rumor) had placed them at Miss Davenant's disposal. But however mythical that statement might be, it was certain that John Crozier, Esq., had sent to New York for a purple velvet-lined carriage (purple was the Circe's color), with fiery, prancing horses, and had driven slowly down the avenue, with Miss Davenant's fair patrician face thrown into strong relief as she leaned against its cushions.

Mrs. Montgomery looked on with complacent interest the while, smiling sagaciously, and saying nothing.

When they had returned home, the evening of the Farnhams' dinner-party, Kate had lingered in the parlor a little while, talking to her aunt about Mr. Crozier.

"Then you don't find him so very insufferable, after all?" her aunt had said, suggestively.

Kate shrugged her shoulders, with a smile, half bored, half contemptuous.

"Not so very insufferable with the billions, you know. But otherwise—" and her large, calm eyes dropped indifferently.

"Don't be so sarcastic," said her aunt. "Once for all, Kate, if he proposes to you again, will you accept him or not? You are nearly twenty years old now, and after twenty it is as well a woman should be married."

Kate's heart gave a fierce bound. Twenty years! What had she done with them? Twenty of the fairest pearls slipped forever from the chain of life that God had given into her hands! Just for that moment it seemed as if the careless words had thrown a flare of light upon her heart, the next the light died away, and left her coldly careless.

"Once for all," she said. "If Mr. Crozier proposes to me again, I will be his wife."

In Carl Seymour's mind there had gradually grown up one predominant feeling of bitter contempt for Kate. Could it be that he had loved such a woman as this all these years? Could such a childhood have grown into such a ripening? He could hardly believe it. He battled against the truth with a fierce, determined trust that was wonderful. But at length the time came when he ceased to dream over little Kathleen's pictures, and shut them out of sight.

Just at the ending of this last month, there was a dark, dreary, foggy day, in which an impulse brought him to a full revelation.

He had been alone in his room all the morning, employing himself in making the preparations necessary before his return to New York. The yellow fog thickened and darkened outside like a heavy curtain drawn by some unseen hand, while the star-faced Clytie rose from her lily cups like a sweet ghost of the summer dreams that were dying away.

Carl did not look at the Clytie often now, and when he did, he only thought of it as a beautiful, cold, dead surface, from which the old charm of truth and soul had fled forever.

Before he had begun his work this morning, he had come to a determination, and now he had finished, he was going to carry it out.

The last picture was laid aside, the last book packed, and there was nothing more to do.

He looked round the room, with a curious lingering in his eyes, at the dead flowers upon the table, at the lily-set Clytie. Then he went out and closed the door behind him. He was going to Bay View.

It was not pleasant walking outside, for the dull October fog hung heavily and drearily before him, almost blinding him. It was a week since he had seen Kate; and when he saw her, she was riding by Mr. Crozier's side, and it was the vague unrest in her eyes that had made him determine to go to her once more, and for the last time. Since the night when she had worn John Crozier's flowers, the breach between her and Carl had widened into a gulf, which seemed almost impassable. In one short month his love for her had changed into bitter distrustfulness. Sometimes he had thought that, even if at last the golden apple was his, it would turn to ashes upon his lips. He hardly intended to ask her for anything this morning; he only wished to bid her good-by; but still, beneath all lay a faint throb of hope, which he did not acknowledge to himself.

When he entered the parlor at Bay View, he found Mrs. Montgomery alone. The mist had almost made the room dark; but the great, glowing fire flung out a warm light, that had a gleam of kindly comfort in itself.

7

Mrs. Montgomery laid her work aside smilingly, and extended her hand to him. She was so glad to see him! Where had he been hiding himself? Visitors were a rarity in these days.

" I have been busy," said Carl, stroking Kate's Italian greyhound on its satiny head. "We 'working-classes' must place business before pleasure, you know."

Mrs. Montgomery took up her work again, ignoring the latter part of the sentence.

"When do you return to New York?" she asked.

"To-morrow," answered Carl. "I came to make my farewells to-day."

"Ah!" quietly responded Mrs. Montgomery, as she sewed. "Then you leave before us. I should have gone last week, but one of Kate's whims detained me."

" Where is Miss Davenant? "

" Enjoying herself somewhere out-of-doors. Imagine such a thing on a day like this. There is no accounting for Kate's fancies. She said she was tired of staying in the house, and so wrapped up and went out."

Carl was silent, and a little stillness fell upon them. The lady's needle glittered in the fire-light like a fairy spear, as it flew backward and forward, but her face was singularly unreadable. She liked this handsome young artist, but she did not like his interference with her plans. To tell the truth, she thought him not a little presumptuous. He had aimed rather too high. Would it not be as well to give him a hint in time? She did not fear for Kate's decision now, but she did not feel quite certain that the path would be so smooth, if this presuming young man became troublesome. She was a business-like woman, and a cool woman, and she went about her work in a cool and business-like manner.

"Has Mr. Crozier called upon you yet?" she asked.

"Mr. Crozier has not called," Carl replied, coolly.

"He was so anxious to see the picture you called 'Kathleen Mavourneen.' They say it is like Kate, you know, and I believe he wished to buy it."

The color rose to Carl's forehead He could understand what this implied, and so answered a little haughtily that the picture was not for sale; that he had painted it with Miss Davenant's kind permission for his own pleasure.

But Mrs. Montgomery received the information very placidly.

"Oh! I beg pardon. You must excuse me, but Mr. Crozier naturally felt a great interest in the picture, you know."

If Carl had not been too thoroughly aroused, he would have been amused; as it was, he refused the inclination to say something rude, and went on stroking Fidele, merely bowing indifferently, and answering,

" Certainly."

But Mrs. Montgomery was not to be baffled. The young man, having made a mistake, must be set right in one way or another; and one plan having failed, it was easy enough to change base.

" Mr. Griffith left Newport few days ago," she said, " I am glad to say."

" Glad to say?" repeated Carl.   " Poor Tom!"

" Perhaps I ought not to have said that; but he was so foolish about Kate.   Of course, he was of a good family, and all that sort of thing, but then he should have known better.   Poor Kate was almost distressed about it.   He bored her to death.   But, you see, women as handsome as she is, generally have little annoyances of that kind."

The blood that had warmed Seymour's face left it colorless, and a spark of contempt lighted his eyes.   This was a phase of treatment that was new to him.   He had met with respect and admiration on all sides; now this calm, business-like woman of the world was trying to show him that his place was not here.

"Of course, you have heard everything before this," the lady went on, placidly. "You see, Mr. Crozier was half engaged to Kate before he went back to China, two years ago, and now she is older—"

Perhaps it was fortunate for Mrs. Montgomery's placidity and Carl's equilibrium that the sentence was broken off, for broken off it was, as the door opened, and Kate, in furs and velvet, made her entrance.

She had not been very brightly tinted at first, but when she caught sight of Carl, all the faint color flew from her face and left it deadly pale. She actually staggered and leaned against the table when she reached it.

"The cold has been too much for me," she explained, in answer to her aunt's surprised inquiry.

"Don't you think you ought to shake hands with me, Mr. Seymour? You are quite a stranger," she said directly, rallying; and she extended her gloved hand with a faint, sweet smile.

Then she seated herself on the lounging-chair by the fire, and leaned back, and Carl had time to see that even the crimson cushions had not glow enough to tinge her white cheeks.

It seemed as though she tried to resist the impulse to meet his eyes at first, but at last she looked up, and tried to chat easily.

"Every one has gone to New York, have they not? Well, summer don't last forever. Mr. Seymour, I wonder if we shall have the pleasure of meeting you in town?"

"In which town?" interposed her aunt. "You know Mr. Crozier spoke of sailing for Paris, Kate."

Kate blushed scarlet, half with embarrassment, half with indignation.

"I meant in New York," she said, with cold brevity, and as her eyes met Carl's, they drooped until the fringes lay upon her cheeks.

It was not the easiest thing in the world to carry on an animated conversation with Mrs. Montgomery's keen eyes fixed upon them; but Kate struggled hard, and kept it from flagging altogether.

Carl could not fail to see the half-impatient contempt with which she met her aunt's diplomatic recurrences to Mr. Crozier, for every mention of his name made her more restless. Before he had watched her long, his bitterness changed to pity. He loved her, and with her sweet face before him, lost his strength.

But how could he speak to her? Mrs. Montgomery held her place, and chatted volubly, with a keen brilliance that would have amused him at any other time, but which now seemed almost unbearable. At last Kate gave up her efforts, and rested in her chair, shading her face with her hand, and looking weary, leaving her conversation-loving relative the task of entertaining their visitor.

Carl resigned himself to his fate in an apathy, contenting himself with an occasional glance at the fair, drooping head and slender hand, and wondering if he must bid her farewell without the last words he had meant to say.

But just in the middle of her aunt's most biting sarcasms, a servant came in and carried her off. A gentleman, a lawyer, the man believed, wished to see her particularly.

Kate did not move for a few seconds after her aunt left the room, but sat looking down at the fur trimming upon her dress, and twisting it nervously with her fingers.

"And so our summer is over at last, Kathleen," said Carl, in a low voice.

The pretty name touched her very soul, but she could only try to steady herself, and lift her tender eyes with a sweet regret in them.

"At last," she said; "but then there are other summers to come, you know."

He rose from his seat and went to her side, bending over her to imprison the restless fingers.

"Are you sure of that?" he asked, hoarsely. "For the last month I have sometimes thought there would be no more summers for me. I came to say good-by to you. Must it be good-by forever? Is it true, this story people tell me, that my innocent, child-love is a false, worldly woman? Is it true, Kathleen Mavourneen?"

She had smiled calmly into other men's eyes, as she sent them to their ruin, but she could not smile at this man. Her beautiful face grew pale, and she slipped from his grasp, and stood up before him with a terrible effort at self-control.

"I do not understand," she faltered. "You have no right to speak to me so. I am—you must know I am engaged, Mr. Seymour—almost a wife, and—and I dare not listen to you." But before she had finished, she dropped her face upon her clasped hands, resting against the mantel-piece, and shivered a little.

Carl gazed at her a moment blankly. Until then he had never known how far he had trusted her, how little he had believed the stories of her worldliness. He drew his hand across his eyes to clear away the blind darkness which seemed to have come upon him, and then he found his voice, and spoke to her.

"Almost a wife!" he repeated. "What right have I

to speak to you of this? What right have I? No right, I suppose. Only the right of a mad fool, who has loved and trusted you, because you were an innocent child once, and the lips I kissed were so pure. Are they pure now, with that man's kisses upon them? If I had not loved you so long, I might forgive you; if I had not loved you in those childish days, I might forget. Kate," he drew near to her, and his voice rung like a command, "lift your sweet face to me, and tell me this is a lie!"

Men who had called him cold-blooded would not have lived through this. His brain whirled, he forgot every-thing but his bitter, bitter passion.

"Kate, lift your sweet face to me, and tell me this is a lie!" he repeated.

She looked up at him proudly, almost defiantly.

She had conquered herself at last; and it was Kate Davenant whose eyes met his, and her voice was as clear as a bell.

"Why do you ask me this?" she said. "What do you mean by lies? I am engaged to Mr. Crozier, and shall be his wife in three months from now. I am very sorry if you have mistaken—" but there the miserable lie she was telling died away before the man's fierce scorn.

"Stop!" he said. "I shall ask no more questions. I

wish to hear nothing more. You 'are sorry I have
mistaken you?' God help me. I would rather have
died two months ago than have believed my love could
end in such utter contempt as I feel now. You have
shown me what a woman can do; you have taught me
whether it is better to trust the face and voice of an angel,
or the lips of a devil. The woman I have loved is dead,
and only you—*you* are left. I came to say farewell to
you. Hear me say it, forever! forever! And hear me
tell you, that I would not touch your hand, or your lips,
if you prayed for it at my feet. The summer is ended,
indeed!"

Men are not merciful at any time, but now, in his wild
despair, this man was worse than cruel. If he had raised
his hand and struck her—struck her on her proud, white
face—he would have been more kind.

Her large eyes opened wide, and purple shadows gathered round them ; her lips parted ; and as he ended, she
swayed a little toward him. But, with a look of ineffable
scorn, he turned and left the room.

Then, and not till then, she slipped like water to the
floor, with her hands flung upward.

CHAPTER X.

AFTER THREE YEARS.

A SPACE of three years! A long leap, you think, but if I had not made it, where would my story have ended? And after these three years have passed, we find ourselves in Mrs. Armadale's parlor, listening to that pretty, fair-faced young matron, as she chats with her brother, counting over the names of the new acquaintances she had made at Saratoga, just before she came to reside at her brother's pretty villa on the Hudson, within an hour and a half of New York by rail. A very sweet, little lady she is, Barbara Armadale. Fair-faced, blonde-haired and clear-eyed, and with three absorbing passions, which fill up her bright, happy, busy life, as a bright, happy, busy young wife and mother. The first of these passions is for "Alf," or more properly Mr. Armadale, who is as bright and cheerful as herself; the next is for the children, whom Mr. Armadale calls "the baby, the little baby, and the least baby of all;" and the last, but not the least, is for her brother, whom she regards as the most perfect human being on earth—next to "Alf." Such

a pretty, cozy, little woman as she looks sitting in the
fire-light, with the shining hair pushed back from her
little pink ears, and the freshness glowing in the rose on
her cheeks.

"Mr. Germaine and his wife, Mr. Vandeleur and his
wife," she says, in a voice like a particularly sweet-tempered robin's, "Mr. Crozier and his wife: and that reminds me, Carl—"

"Mr. Who and his wife?" interrupted a voice from the
dark corner where the sofa stood.

"Mr. Crozier and his wife," answered Mrs. Armadale.
"And, as I said, that reminds me, Carl, that I wanted to
ask you if you knew Mr. Crozier. He said he met you
several times when he was at Newport, the summer before
your uncle died and left you your fortune."

The man she spoke to was lying upon the sofa, stretched
at full length, with his hands thrown upward and clasped
above his head, and as his sister turned round to him the
fire-light fell full upon his face. A very handsome face
it was, clear-cut and large-eyed, the mouth half hidden
by a heavy, down-drooping, blond moustache.

But, handsome as it was, a keen physiognomist would
have hesitated to pronounce it perfect. It looked like a
face which the world's influences had spoiled, or, rather, it

looked as if its owner was a man to whom the wine of life had turned bitter. The clear, perfectly-shaped eyes wore a careless, sarcastic expression, the mouth was wearied and bored and not unlike the eyes in its indifferent satire.

"Yes, I met him several times. Something between a professional prize-fighter and a banker's clerk, wasn't he?"

Mrs. Armadale laughed.

"Well, he wasn't very aristocratic-looking, to be sure. A little 'mushroomy,' one might say; but he was immensely rich. Horridly rich, I thought. One of those people who cannot help showing how rich they are."

"I know him," said Carl. "They used to call him the Grand Mogul. Barbara," with a curious biting of his lips which the firelight showed, "didn't you say something about Mrs. Crozier?"

"Yes. His wife was with him."

"What sort of a woman was she?"

"Pretty," said Barbara; "a trifle faded and worn, but still pretty. I often thought it was no wonder she had faded with John Crozier, Esq., for a husband. He was so abominably dictatorial. I should want to bite a man who spoke to me in the authoritative style he used to her. But what made you ask about her?"

"I saw her at Newport," was the brief reply. "She was a belle then, and there was quite a little furore created when she engaged herself to the Mogul; but it was the old story, you know—exchange and barter."

Little Mrs. Barbara shrugged her plump shoulders contemptuously.

"I'm not sorry for her, then. How *can* women? I think it's horrible."

"You are a different woman to Mrs. Crozier," said the gentleman, indifferently. "Let us talk of something else, Barbie."

Strange to say, the lady was not so much interested in the subject, but that she could easily leave it. Other people's business rarely interested Mrs. Armadale, and she passed on to something else. · "The children," were the next topic. She knew Carl always liked to hear about them, and now she wanted his advice particularly.

"You see, I don't know what to do," she said, with a little doubtful anxiety that was wonderfully motherly and pretty on her almost girlish face. "I can't be with them always, and I don't like to trust them to the servants altogether. Old aunt Dorcas is very good, but the children are so apt to adopt her funny, negro *patois;* and besides, if Clara and Johnny don't begin French now, they never *will* acquire the accent."

"Terrible!" said her brother, with amused laziness. "What a fearful state of affairs in the nursery dominion. Barbara, you are like a domesticated robin, always in a flutter about the nest."

"There is a great deal of anxiety about a family," with a demure sententiousness, which was the most delightful little face in the world. "You have never been married, Carl."

"No," said Carl, meditatively. "I should have been a better man if I had. If there had been a woman true and loving enough to be my wife and share my lot, I should have been nearer heaven than I am now;" and the fire-light showed the handsome, bitten lip again; and Barbara wondered somewhat at the bitter sigh that ended the sentence.

"Well," she said softly, "I don't see why you didn't get married, dear. You are not poor, and I am sure any woman might love you."

"I am not poor now," was the quiet reply. "I was not rich when nothing but money would have won the woman I loved. But what about the children?"

Barbara's blue eyes opened softly. Was it possible that

her famous, handsome brother had been disappointed? She had never suspected it before. How had it happened? How could it have happened?

But she was a wise, good little woman, and understood this handsome brother well enough to know that he would think it kinder if she let the accidental remark slip by without any comment.

"Well," she went on, "I thought if we had a governess. Don't you think it would be nice if I could find some elegant, accomplished woman? I should feel so much more comfortable."

"'If' you could, I think it would be a good plan. Have you spoken to Alf about it?'

"Yes; but I wanted to ask your opinion. If I had been in my own house it would have been different," laughing frankly; "but I did not know whether you would like the idea of a 'correct' lady to criticise you."

"I don't think she will criticise me," said Carl. "The cherubs will occupy all her attention. What are you listening at so intently? Is it Alf at last?"

"I thought I heard somebody coming," coloring a little and laughing. "Yes, it is Alf at last. I hear him speaking to Roberts now. Excuse me a minute."

Carl smiled as she jumped up with the bright, pleased

look on her face, and went out to meet her husband, who
was returning from his daily trip to New York, for he
was a lawyer in a fine business. This sweet-tempered little
sister of his always amused him. She was so affectionate
and merry, so loving and womanly over the children, so
prettily solicitous about this same good-natured Alf's
comfort. Always so tender and impulsive, even now,
after eight years of married life, when the honey-moon in
some cases would have been only a bright spot lying far
in the darkness, bringing tears into the aching eyes that
dared to look backward. But Barbara Armadale was just
the little woman whose honey-moon would never pass,
because it had been a honey-moon whose brightness had
been the brightness of her own sunny sweetness and affectionate temperament. To this day "Alf" was the Alf of
the bridal tour, not quite as sentimental, of course, (perhaps happily,) but still quite as careful of Mrs. Armadale,
and quite as implicitly believed in by Mrs. Armadale, as
when for four successive weeks they had regarded earthly
food as something entirely unworthy of consideration, and
had caught terrible and very unromantic colds by persist-
ently gazing at the moon and quoting Byron and Moore. In
Mrs. Armadale's mind there was but one thing on earth
to equal Alf, and that one thing was the baby, and the

8

only things which could come up to them both were the
other two children.

Carl—this bitter Carl Seymour—you know him by this
time, I am sure, who was hard and sarcastic, careless, and
often selfish in these sad, embittered days, cared for this
loving young wife and mother as he cared for no one else.
She made him better and purer, and exerted an influence
upon him such as even he himself never dreamed of.
Sometimes at night, as he had passed the open nursery-
door, he had looked in upon her as she sat in the low
rocking-chair with baby on her breast, and grave, blue-
eyed Johnny kneeling before her in his white night-gown,
saying after her slowly the old, never dying, never fading,
"Our Father."   And then, after he had watched them
for a moment, he had turned away, feeling a little nearer
heaven for the sound of the childish prayer.

The world said of him, and said truly, that he was a
selfish, brilliant, cynical man, who had won fame, who
was rich, and who cared little for people in general.   Men
with fresh hearts avoided, while they admired him;
women, who were true-hearted, pitied him for his lost life
and bitterness.   Lavish he was and generous to profuse-
ness, seeming to value his wealth lightly, yet always cold
and cynical, sneering at the best impulses of men and

women, flinging out stinging sarcasms mingled with his graceful wit. Not a bad man—never that—always an honorable gentleman, but nevertheless a man who could hardly look forward, and dare not look back. Barbara had only known him as her brother and her friend, talented, graceful, popular, and to her always kindly and tender. She had thought him a little satirical sometimes, but that was all.

"It is only Carl's way," she had said, and gone on worshipping him.

A good woman might have made him a good man. A woman who was neither good nor true had, as we know, reader, made him what he was.

He lay back on the couch when Barbara left him, and closed his eyes. He could hear her fresh voice in the hall as she greeted her husband; and then came the little pause that was suggestive of the kiss the gentleman always received after a day's absence. Then the two went upstairs together, and a chorus from Johnny and Clara broke out as they passed the nursery door.

If such a kiss might have greeted him; if such a bright face had met him each night; if such childish voices had shouted his name. The thought passed through his mind, leaving a dull pain.

He did not love Kate Davenant now. Sometimes he thought he hated her, but still, under all his contempt, lay the old scar throbbing, throbbing. Three years, and she was faded and worn, and this man, who was her master and owner, was proving that he knew his power. Could it be? A faint disgust thrilled him.

As he lay there with closed eyes, the four summer months passed before him again. The first evening when Alice Farnham had pointed out the " Circe," as she smiled on the celebrities with the glow in her purple eyes. Then the times when he had met her again and again, always the belle, always with the wonderful grace that drew the world after her. Then the days when he had looked up from his work at the star-faced Clytie, and unconsciously gained inspiration.

He could see again the vaporous folds of muslin that trailed on the balcony, the intense light on the bright, glinting hair, and the intense soft scarlet on cheek and lip. He could almost hear the whisper of the sea again as the exquisite voice floated back to him. He had not forgotten— ah! could he ever forget! La Valliere kneeling in the dim, mellow light, with the white uplifted face and passionate eyes, while the convent-bell broke upon her praying, with its dooming knell. And then the moon was shining on little Kathleen's scarlet cloak, as she sung her song with the softness of tears veiling her voice. Ah! the eyes he had met that night, the true, tender eyes, true and tender for that moment, as they drooped before his gaze. Could it all—all have ended in this heartless life of his, in which he was told that the woman he had loved and trusted, the woman who had blighted his very soul, had won the prize for which she had lost all, and now in wearing it was faded and worn? All his hatred and contempt died away in an aching longing for the trust he had once felt in his innocent child-love. He had not forgiven her, he thought he never could; but, ah! if the dead past could have come back again.

At least an hour he lay pondering, until the flame died out of the fire, and left nothing but the red embers, shedding a rich, gloomy light about the room. But at last the nursery-door opened, and Mrs. Armadale and her husband came down again, talking and laughing.

"Gone to sleep, Carl?" Barbara asked, gayly. "No? How dark you are. I am going to ring for lights and tea." And she pulled the bell.

When tea was brought in, she seated herself at the head of the table in the sunshiniest of moods. She cut the cold tongue for Alf, and made the thinnest of sandwiches for him, calling him lazy all the time, but still looking as if she enjoyed it. Carl liked one lump of sugar, didn't he, and Alf three? Baby had cut his first little tooth— the darling? and Clara could say her prayers without being told, and Johnny had called his papa "Alf, dear," because he heard mamma say it. To all of which chatter the two gentlemen listened with laughing attention. The little lady did not detail nursery gossip to every one, but she knew that Carl and Alf liked it.

"And the best of all is yet to be told," she went on. "Alf has really found a governess, Carl."

"What sort of a governess? Fossil specimen, or otherwise?"

"Most decidedly 'otherwise,'" said Alf. "I am not going to describe her, because description would be superfluous; and besides, there is a curious coincidence, which I wish to surprise you with, as it did me."

"But she speaks French?" suggested Barbara.

"And German and Italian," answered Alf. "I won't answer for Japanese and High Dutch, and I ain't quite certain about Gallic and Hindoostanee; but I am quite safe about the rest."

"Pianist?" queried Mrs. Armadale again.

"Pianist, organist, violinist, banjoist, plays on the bagpipes, dances on a tight-rope, does up *trapeze* performance, sings comic songs."

"Now, Alf," from Mrs. Armadale, "do be quiet and answer one more question. What church—"

"Ah!" interrupted her husband, gravely, "as to that, I believe she is a Protestant; but, being a very accommodating young lady, I dare say she would have no objection to changing her religion. Mohammedan for Johnny, Mormonism for Clara, and Hardshell Baptist for the cherubim. Anything else, my dear?"

Mrs. Armadale shook her head.

"No. I am quite satisfied; but what is her name?"

Alf stopped half way to his mouth with a sandwich.

"The mischief! I forgot to ask her, or else it has slipped my memory. Wait a minute, now I remember. It is something beginning with David— Never mind quizzing, Barbie. You will see her to-morrow."

It was some time before Mr. Armadale could be brought to a due sense of the solemnity of the question discussed; but at last Mrs. Armadale managed him and learned the particulars.

A young lady had replied to his advertisement in person. An aristocratic-looking girl, with a magnificent, proud face, and bright-brown hair.

"Such a voice!" said the gentleman. "It was like the echo of a song; and such a perfect accent of both French and German. She says she has spent several years in Europe. She must have a history. It is an easy matter to see that she was never educated for a governess. There s so much superb ease about her manner."

"How fortunate!" said delighted Barbara. "I want the children to learn the languages by ear, and you know we can't afford to go to Europe for a year or so. I am so glad, Alfred."

"I knew you would be," he answered. "But let us have some music, my dear. I am going to smoke, and want my evening sonata."

It was eleven o'clock before the music was over; and then Carl went to his studio, for he still painted, and holding up a taper, looked at two pictures that hung side by side, the two pictures painted three years before at New-port. Brown-haired, purple-eyed, and rare-faced, with the exquisite sweetness and flawless charm. And this woman was "faded and worn!"

The light flashed over the fair, still features, and then they were shadowed in darkness; and he turned away and left them to go to his room and dream of a strange woman, who was the new governess, and yet wore Kate Davenant's face, and spoke with Kate Davenant's voice.

CHAPTER XI.

A SURPRISE.

ALL the next day he was in his studio, busy, adding the finishing touches to a picture; and as at such times he never left his work, he heard nothing more of his sister's arrangements. But when at night, after laying everything aside, he was coming down to the parlor, he met Mrs. Armadale descending from the nursery, with the little pink-faced bundle of white lawn and lace in her arms, which always suggested baby, and she stopped him on the landing with a delighted face.

"Are you coming into the parlor now? I hope so. She has come, Carl, and I like her ever so much. I know we shall be good friends."

Carl smiled. He knew it would be the stranger's fault if they were not. The idea of Barbara's not being good friends with anybody was rather a joke. She had such a habit of purring, and cooing, and petting, that not the most stony of stony hearts could have resisted her. Carl followed her down-stairs, and on their way she dilated eloquently on her new acquaintance. The new governess was so elegant, and so beautiful, and, "oh, Carl, *so* sweet!"

Mrs. Armadale was sure she should love her like a sister. The new governess had won the children's hearts at first, and Mrs. Armadale was just bringing baby down to be exhibited.

"You see," went on the kind-hearted little matron, "I want to make her feel at home, Carl. She seems so lonely. She has neither mother, nor father, nor relations of any kind. The aunt, who educated her, has been dead only a few months. Of course, one can't ask questions, but I am sure she is a gentlewoman born. She is so aristocratic-looking."

"What is her name?" asked Carl. "Have you found out yet, or did you engage her on the strength of her aristocracy?"

"No," laughed Mrs. Armadale, settling baby's flowing robes preparatory to entering the parlor. "I am wiser than Alf. Her name is as aristocratic as her face. Davenant—Kate Davenant. Ain't it pretty? Open the door, please." And as Carl bent over her, and turned the handle, a sweet, low ripple of laughter came upon them, and they stepped into the room.

Some one sat beside the fire, in an easy-chair, talking to

Mr. Armadaie, who was listening, with entranced pleasure showing itself on every feature. The back of the chair was turned toward the door, but Carl could see the folds of a black dress lying upon the carpet, and a close-fitting sleeve setting off a smooth, round wrist and slender hand, which rested upon the chair-arm.

At the sound of the door opening the lady looked up, and Barbara came forward into the light of the fire with baby.

"My brother, Mr. Seymour, Miss Davenant," she said, smiling. "And here is baby—"

Miss Davenant rose in the firelight, the crimson glow falling full upon her, upon the trailing folds of the black dress sweeping upon the carpet with the old royal sweep of the Circe's robes, upon the crown of glinting brown hair, with its metallic sheen, upon the "Valliere" face, and the winy purple of the eyes that met Carl Seymour's. Just a glance from either face, and these two who had loved each other once, whose lives had once seemed linked together, met with a calm bow as strangers, not touching hands, hardly smiling, unless the half sneer on the man's face could be called a smile.

"And this is baby?" said Miss Davenant, turning to the lawn and lace in Mrs. Armadale's arms. "Is baby one of my pupils?"

It was quite a serene face that smiled the old, sweet smile over Barbara's treasure—a face much more serene than Carl Seymour's.   He had turned away with a bitter smile by no means pleasant to see.   And so Mrs. Crozier was not Miss Davenant, and this girl had crossed his path again?

To think that such a woman should live in innocent Barbara's home, and have the care of innocent Barbara's children!   As he watched her bend over and kiss the baby lips, he felt a thrill of anger.   There was all the old grace in her every movement, all the old fascination in the perfect face, but their charm was lost to Carl.   If he had known all, he might not have been so harsh.   Knowing only what he did—that she had proved false and mercenary, and had been his ruin—there was nothing, nothing of forgiveness or relenting in his mind.

Innocent Barbara was in a seventh heaven of good-natured delight.   This beautiful girl so. ardently appreciated baby.   When at last Miss Davenant acceded to Alf's request and went to the piano, the little lady drew her chair to her brother's side.

"Did you ever see such a curious coincidence, Carl? That 'La Valliere' and the 'Kathleen Mavourneen' are the very reproductions of her face.   Is it possible you have ever met her before?"

"It is a coincidence I cannot account for," said the gentleman, briefly. "I can hardly believe it, but this Miss Davenant of yours is the young lady who was pointed out to me at Newport as Mr. Crozier's future wife, and until I saw her to-night, I imagined she was the Mrs. Crozier you met at Saratoga."

"You don't say so? Oh, no! My Mrs. Crozier was a little, brown-haired woman, with a harassed face and a scared expression. As unlike Miss Davenant as it is possible for two women to be. The engagement must have been broken. What a voice she has! Do listen to her!"

She was singing a little song she had sung for Carl a hundred times before. A little Spanish love-song, with an accompaniment like running water, and a faint throb. of pain threading through it. Carl did not like to hear it now. He would gladly have closed his ears to it, and yet he must sit and listen to the end, and hear Barbara's ecstatic chorus of "Beautiful!"

But at length baby fell asleep, and Barbara carried him to the nursery, and a few minutes after sent for Alf to come up-stairs. Alf made his excuses and went. It was possible that Johnny had a cough, or Clara's face was flushed, and under such circumstances a grave consultation must be held.

After he had left them, Kate rose from her seat at the piano and came to the fire. It was not a pleasant situation to be in, but she carried herself gracefully and calmly as usual. Carl looked at her from head to foot. Faded and worn! Twenty years would hardly change her! Every tint on her deliate skin was as rarely vivid and firm as the rose and pearl of a sea-shell. Just as much the Circe now, when she was only Mrs. Armadale's governess, as when she had been in Mrs. Montgomery's charge and the belle of Newport.

" I had no idea—" she began, and then faltered a little under his cold eyes, and stopped.

" Nor had I," was the icy reply. "I wonder if either of us are very agreeably surprised! "

The color ran up on her face, but the eyes turned toward him showed nothing but calm, well-bred surprise at his sarcastic bitterness. His love had been worse than indifference, for it had robbed her of his respect. He was almost savage in his cynicism, and he had so far lost his reverence for her that he forgot himself, and felt as though there would be some merited revenge in baffling her proud stateliness with scorn. But this was not an easy matter.

" I am afraid not," she said, in answer to his sarcasm. " But I do not see how we—how I, at least—can help it.

If I had known, I certainly should not have come here. As it is, unless you tell Mrs. Armadale to send me away, I suppose I shall have to bear my share of the unpleasantness."

It was very quietly said, almost meekly, indeed, but the words and tone stung him to the quick. It was a hard task to abuse a woman who was at his mercy, and yet showed that she felt no fear, even while she knew her helplessness.

" Tell Mrs. Armadale to send you away ! " he sneered. " Do you think I am a brute? My experience has not made me a very good man, or a very chivalrous one. You see I have outlived my tender belief in ' ministering angels,' etc.; and I am not very polite to women whom I neither love nor respect. I told you I would never forgive you— and I never will. You have made me what I am, but as for the rest—"

He stopped and shrugged his shoulders contemptuously.

Kate Davenant took one step nearer, and looked at him fearlessly. She had got over the days when his harsh words had made her faint at his feet, and his almost insulting and quite unmanly tone roused her. It was a horribly bitter thing to hear him speak of " women whom he neither loved nor respected," but her indignation helped her to bear it.

"I am very poor, Mr. Seymour," she said, clearly and steadily. "I have not one friend or protector in the world. I am a menial in your house, and I suppose I am at your mercy; but I have not asked you to forgive me yet. When I ask you, it will be time to refuse pardon, not till then."

For the first time in these three years he felt as if he ought to respect this girl. She was not afraid of him, and she had not forgotten herself, as he had. He knew she was saying to him just what he deserved to hear, and so he was silent, and let her go on.

"I don't think it is necessary we should be enemies," she said. "I should have begun no warfare. I was content to let the dead past bury its dead. If you think proper to tell Mrs. Armadale that I shall not stay in your house (it is your house, I hear), you may do so. As to your being a brute, I did not call you one; but I don't know exactly what I ought to call a man who insults a woman, who, if she has even wronged him, is still a woman, and has no power to retaliate."

Her white throat was arched, and her eyes opened wide with a great spark of starry fire in them, as she looked down upon him. There was not a touch of weakness or regretful yielding in her whole being, he could see that. It was a matter of open conflict between powers equal, though one was even a woman. Greek had met Greek at last, and now came the tug of war. A little fiery thrill shot through the man's veins. It was remembrance, it was resentment, it was admiration. She was so beautiful! so beautiful! so proudly perfect; and then—it might have been. Still he answered her as defiantly as she had spoken.

"Thank you!" he said. "You are very kind. And as you are so mercifully disposed, suppose we let matters rest here. I myself see no reason for heroics, in spite of my little impoliteness. I forgot myself. Pray, excuse me."

Kate bowed. Just such a bow, haughty and tolerant, as had won her a reputation in by-gone days. Then she seated herself, and taking up Barbara's neglected tatting, began to work industriously. Mr. Seymour had not shaken her self-possession in the least. There was no trace of either anger or agitation in her face, and when Mrs. Armadale returned, Kate was still employing herself with the flying shuttle, with an appearance of ease and pleasure, which delighted the young matron immensely.

The next day the children were taken in hand. Johnny, the youngest pupil, was a blue-eyed urchin, with a wonderful good-nature and gravity, that made him, in a small

9

way, quite a character.   After a few minutes' calm inspec-
tion, with his hands clasped behind his back, he made an
unconditional surrender to Miss Davenant's witchery, and
said his lessons, gazing fixedly and wonderingly at her
beautiful face.   One glance won graceful, quiet little
Clara.   She was a second Barbara, with all her mother's
innate refinement and passionate admiration of beauty.
From the date of the first kiss, Miss Davenant reigned
supreme.

Mrs. Armadale, as I have said before, was not curious,
but it must be admitted the new governess interested her
deeply.   How in the world could the belle of Newport
have fallen into this position?   But Carl was strangely
reticent on the subject.   He only spoke of her as an
acquaintance by reputation, and never hinted that he had
ever spoken to her before.   Besides, he did not seem at
all anxious to pursue the subject; indeed, once or twice
she fancied that he avoided it.

CHAPTER XII.

GOVERNESS AND FRIEND.

IT was not often that Mrs. Armadale looked troubled, but troubled she certainly looked, when she came into the school-room to Kate, one morning, a month or so after the arrival of the governess. Mr. Armadale had returned from New York only the night before. in a great hurry.

"I don't know what to do, Kate," she said, after the children had been sent down-stairs. "Mr. Armadale says it is absolutely imperative that I should go to New Orleans with him. There has been some trouble about the property there, which Clara's godmother left her, and my presence is necessary. It seems I must sign something. How can I leave the children? Baby is not well, and both Johnny and Clara are ailing. I shall be perfectly miserable, though, of course, I won't say so to Alf. Besides, it will be so unpleasant for you."

Kate had not meant to be selfish, but, honestly, the first idea which had suggested itself to her was the unpleasant position she would necessarily be thrown into. But Barbara's evident anxiety roused her sympathies.

"You have no need to be anxious," she said, cheerfully. "Aunt Dorcas is reliable, I think ; and though I am not a very good nurse, I will try to take care of the children."

"I am sure you will do that," answered Barbara, her face clearing slightly. "But I am afraid it will be so much trouble; and then Clara is so delicate that I am always anxious if there is a tinge too much or too little on her cheeks. I wish—I do wish the journey was not so positively necessary."

It required all Kate's powers of consolation to reassure her ; but at last she became somewhat less fearful.

"But if any of them should be taken sick," she said, as she left the room to go and superintend her packing, "be sure to write to me at once, if you please."

Kate promised faithfully, and the young matron took her departure in a somewhat easier frame of mind. As for the Circe, to say that she was perplexed would be to give but a faint idea of her feelings. The children she could have managed easily; nay, she said to herself, if there had been three dozen instead of three, she would gladly have undertaken their charge, if by doing so she could have avoided this embarrassing *tête-à-tête* position. But it seemed there was no avoiding it, and so she could only accept it with as good a grace as possible.

Since the first evening she had hardly once seen her antagonist alone. When they had met, they had barely exchanged civilities. How would *tête-à-tête* dinners and breakfasts pass off, for necessarily Miss Davenant must take the place Mrs. Armadale had vacated? In spite of her discomfort, she could not help smiling as she thought of it. Well, there was only one part which could be acted, and that involved perfect, well-bred calmness. Since she must meet him, and play the part of mistress of the household, it should be done gracefully, and without her manner indicating that anything had occurred to make the position other than a pleasant one. Nevertheless, she felt it would need all her self-possession and self-knowledge to carry her through.

The day was a busy one, and rather unsettled by the preparations for the journey; but at last the bustle was over, and the carriage containing Mrs. Armadale was driven away, with that anxious young matron's face showing itself at the window, in a rather dubiously cheerful farewell to the children.

When it was out of sight, Kate took Johnny and Clara by the hand and led them into the parlor.

It had been one of those chilly, gray days, with which the early part of autumn is occasionally interspersed, and a fire had been in the room all day, and by this fire Mr. Seymour was seated as they entered. He had not expected their coming, it was very plain; but Kate led her young charges to the hearth with the calmest of faces.

"The children will take tea with us to-night, if you have no objection, Mr. Seymour," she said, serenely, as she rested her arched foot on the fender to warm. "I thought they might possibly feel lonely."

Perhaps he was a little more mercifully inclined than usual; at all events, he took her cue as calmly as it was given. His quiet reply was quite a relief to Kate, for, to tell the truth, her courage had oozed out at her finger-ends when she first observed his presence. So far so good. At least the enemy had acknowledged the flag of truce. She took a seat opposite to him, and began to talk easily as she worked upon Mrs. Armadale's tatting. Mrs. Armadale had said she would, probably, be absent two weeks: did he think it probable her stay would be prolonged? Mr. Seymour thought it just possible. Ah! that was a pity—she had been so anxious about the children. Barbara always was anxious about the children, was the gentleman's reply; and by this time his book lay upon his knee, half-closed upon his shapely hand, and he was watching Miss Davenant's slim, pointed fingers, as they flew back and forth with the little pearl shuttle.

She knew he was looking at her, and the knowledge was not pleasant. Nevertheless she did not care to look up, and so went on quietly.

"You were reading when we came in," with a faint smile. "Don't let us disturb you. The children will be quiet."

"Thank you!" he said, as serenely, yet with a keen scrutiny in his haughty, handsome eyes. "There is no fear of disturbance. Listen to what I was reading:

"'I think, in the lives of most women and men,
  There are times when all might be smooth and even,
 If the dead could only find out when
  To come back to us and be forgiven.'

"I was wondering," he went on, "if this verse might not mean more than dead friends. Might we not apply it to dead loves, dead hopes, dead happiness?"

If Miss Davenant had been an unsophisticated young lady she would probably have blushed and shown uneasiness under this seemingly harmless remark, which, with the old story in the past, might be so pointed; but as she was not an unsophisticated young lady, she did not blush, but merely drew out the tiny shuttle a little faster, with a soft, calm laugh. `

"Possibly," she said. "But as I have neither dead hopes nor dead loves, I cannot say, you see. But what a beautiful verse it is! Won't you please read me the rest?"

Checkmate! She had secured her draw-bridge; but even years after she did not forget the spark of slow fire in his eyes, as they fell upon the book again.

For the first time, in the evening, the red shot warmly to her very forehead, and she bent over her work to hide it.

He read on for an hour, passing from one poem to another, hardly looking up from the book, and seeming all the time to be acting from a sense of cold politeness. Before the tea-tray was brought in, Kate was not quite sure but that his face wore a slightly bored expression, and she made an indignant resolve to confine herself to the school-room and nursery as much as possible.

There was a faint crimson spot on either cheek when at last she took her place at the head of the table, with Johnny and Clara on either side, and her enemy as *vis-à-vis*. She looked very graceful in her position, Carl thought, and very sweet, with her soft-voiced commands to the children; but she did not look at him more than she could help; and once, when handing him his cup, her hand touched his, she flushed like a girl, and drew it away quickly. For her part she was wondering if the meal would ever be over, and asking herself if it would be too glaring, hereafter, to leave him with his housekeeper, and stop with the children in the nursery. Two weeks of this would be impossible! But it was over at length, and she rose from the table and touched the bell.

"We will go up to the nursery now," she said, to the children. "You know we have to finish that story, Johnny." And with her two charges running before her, in a great hurry for the story, she went out of the room and closed the door behind her.

Once up-stairs, she found her hands full. Baby was there, with aunt Dorcas, fretting a little as he lay on her lap. Johnny and Clara seated themselves on their respective stools, anxious for the promised story; but Kate had been long enough in the Armadale household to feel a trifle anxious at baby's flushed face, and faint little grunts of disapproval.

"What is the matter with him?" she asked of aunt Dorcas. "I hope he isn't sick, aunty?"

The old woman shook her head.

"I'm afeard he ain't well, honey," she said. "He's bin sorter gruntin' all day. Mebbe he's only missin' his mar."

Kate held out her hands.

"Let me have him," she said, with a faint sense of discomfort. "I hope he won't be sick while Mrs. Armadale is away."

She felt uneasy, and she could hardly hide it. What if anything should happen! She held baby closer in her arms, and bent and kissed its little face. She looked wonderfully like Barbara about her tender mouth and anxious eyes as she did it. She had always loved the children, even in her bitterest moments, and it seemed so natural for her heart to warm with the soft cheeks nestling against it. The children had their story, and after it came to its natural ending, where the youngest brother did all the impossible things, and married the obliging princess with the convenient father and three kingdoms, she sent them to bed.

Aunt Dorcas went with them. Kate was left to herself, seated on Barbara's rocking-chair, with Barbara's baby on her lap. She hardly knew what she was thinking of, as she rocked to and fro, and sung one of Barbara's pretty songs in her low, clear voice—the voice that had brought showers of flowers to her feet in by-gone days. But, at any rate, she was thinking deeply, for her eyes were fixed dreamily on the fire, and she did not hear the quick footstep coming up the stairs. There was a footstep, and just by the open door it stopped a moment, and Carl Seymour drew his breath sharply as he looked in. What was there of good or evil, in this girl, that she could sting him with her cool indifference and bitter pride, and then come among these innocent children and teach them to love her as if she were as innocent as themselves? And hold this white-souled baby in her arms, and sing tender songs to it with that tender smile on her lips? And then a wild thought leaped up. What if the past had been only a dream! What if God and heaven (for it seemed as if God and heaven were near to the tender vision) had but given him the right to call this girl wife, and to enter the little room and kiss her sweet face, and hold her white hands, and draw her head upon his shoulder, feeling at rest, and better and stronger for her lovingness! Ah! how his heart beat as he remembered how far apart they were, and how they were to live their lives away from each other and unforgiven. But when she came to the end of her little song, he turned away.

It seemed as if there was a spell upon them that night,

or that Fate had ordered that the sea of memory should be stirred, for once again their acted part was broken in upon.

Baby had fallen asleep, and after laying him in the cradle, Kate had left him to aunt Dorcas, and gone down-stairs to give some directions to the servants.

Having done what she wished, she intended retiring for the night; but on reaching the head of the stairs, she found the servants had neglected to lower the lights of a large swinging-lamp which had its place there. It must be attended to, and balancing herself upon one foot, she reached over the balustrade to touch it.

She heard some one close the parlor-door as she did so, and glancing down, caught sight of Carl coming up to-ward her.   Perhaps it was her confusion, perhaps the light dazzled her, but, at least, she could not see well, and her hand was unsteady.   He was only a few steps below her, and in an impatient impulse she bent further over, lost her balance, and then her foot slipped, and but that he had caught her in his arms, she would have fallen down the whole flight.   As it was, his arm closed strongly round her waist, and for a moment she rested upon his breast, crimson with mortification.   The next instant he had released her, and she stood upon the step feeling almost indignant, and, in spite of herself, trembling from head to foot, and showing her confusion terribly. For him, he was the calmest of the two, but his face was perfectly colorless, and his voice sounded almost unnatural when he spoke to her.

"I hope you are not hurt!" he said. "It was fortunate I happened to come when I did."

She could hardly answer him. It seemed so horrible to her. Her cheek had touched his as she fell. And this man had loved her once, and now hated her!

"No," she said, "I am not hurt. Thank you!" and before he had time to speak, she had turned and gone swiftly up the stairs again, hardly knowing what she did.

Her cheeks were hot, scarlet, when she locked her door, and went to the mirror to look at herself, and her mouth was trembling like a child's. She almost clenched her hand in her passion of humiliation. She could not control herself, and after the first glance, she dropped her face upon her hands.

"Oh! I am a coward!" she said, passionately. "Oh! what a pitiful coward I am! What is this I am learning? What have I done?"

CHAPTER XIII.

THE BEGINNING OF A SECOND LOVE.

KATE dressed herself very slowly the next morning, and stood a long time at the mirror, before she could decide to go down to the breakfast-room at all. Not that she was anxious about her toilet, but that she wished to put off the evil hour as long as possible, if not forever. The bell had rung for the second time. Even then a sudden recollection caused her to turn back to the dressing-table. There had been a slender chain round her neck the night before, suspending a little Gothic cross of onyx and gold, and it had suddenly struck her that she had not seen it since she dressed. She could not recollect having taken it off, and it certainly was not on the toilet-stand. Perhaps it had dropped upon the floor. She bent down and looked for it, but to no avail; it was not to be found. Her grandmother had given her the cross the day she left with Mrs. Montgomery, and had told her that it was her father's gift to her deserted mother. She had worn it often in the Newport days, and once she had told Carl

Seymour its story, and he had asked her if the mother's true heart had descended to the daughter.

It might possibly have slipped from its clasp as she fell, and he might have picked it up. That was the only way in which she could account for its absence, and she by no means liked the idea of recalling the scene to his mind by questioning him. Surely, if he had seen it, he would restore it without being asked.

Giving up the search as useless, she went down to the nursery for Clara and Johnny, who were waiting for her to take them to the breakfast-room.

Aunt Dorcas, who was crooning over baby, looked up somewhat anxiously as she entered. Baby was lying quite still, his tiny face flushed with the hot-red, which Kate knew was Mrs. Armadale's special horror, and she felt a nervous thrill as she noted the dark rings round his eyes, and the heavy sleep he seemed to have fallen into.

"Is he worse?" she asked, quickly. "How did he sleep, aunt Dorcas?"

"Mighty badly, Miss Kate, honey. He's jest dropped off for the first time since twelve last night, and mebbe it will help him. Sleep does a power o' good to chil'en."

Mrs. Armadale surely never looked more anxious than her governess did, as she stooped over the little one, and touched its hot cheek with her white forefinger. It was just pretty Barbara's way, and there was just pretty Barbara's thoughtfulness in her softened eyes.

"Well," she said, when she raised her head, "I must go down to breakfast now, but if baby is no better soon, I shall send for the doctor."

She marshalled the children before her into the parlor, talking to them gayly: but for all that, she found it no easy matter to say her good-morning. Her face colored high, in spite of herself, and her hand positively shook as she poured out the first cup of coffee. For a while Carl and she had exchanged places, for, though he was a shade paler than usual, he was quite collected.

"We may expect a letter from Barbara to-day, I suppose," he said, with a slight smile. "When she is away I am always compelled to issue bulletins from the nursery, on pain of seeing her worn to a skeleton by the time Alf brings her home."

Kate was not quite sure but that she felt grateful to him for his nonchalance. But then he could afford to be nonchalant. It was not he who had fallen into her arms, and her cheeks grew a thought hotter than before.

"I am afraid the bulletin for to-day is not very satisfactory," she said, trifling with her spoon. " Baby is not well this morning." And before she had finished her sentence, she found herself coloring again, for he was smiling. With his recollection of the Circe of Newport, with her train of celebrities, and her butterfly-life, it seemed so odd to see her sitting there, in her quiet dress, and with her mermaiden's hair knotted in the plain school-room fashion. A novel position for the Circe, surely, this of nurse, and consoler, and deputy mamma.

He was sorry to hear it, he said to her. She must not allow herself to be frightened; but, if she thought it necessary, he would send for the family physician.

"Thank you. I will wait until evening," she answered. "If I still feel doubtful then, I will let you know."

She was glad when the meal was over, and she found herself rising from the table.

But before she left the room, a servant came in to remove the breakfast things, and Kate thought there could hardly be a better time for speaking of her lost ornament, and so mentioned it.

"I had it, last night," she added, addressing the servant, "I might have dropped it upon the stairs."

But the girl had not seen it, and Mr. Seymour said nothing, only when first she spoke, Kate observed that he raised his eyes from the paper he was reading. How-

10

ever, she gained no information, and so must fain go up-
stairs, and leave the cross to its fate.

What a dull day that was! The sky was dull, the
house was dull, the children were dull, and Kate herself
was in a perfect fit of blues. The lessons did not make
any progress at all. Johnny's head ached, he said, and
poor little Clara looked pale. Before the morning had
half passed, Kate closed the books.

"We won't try any more to-day, children," she said.
"We must cure that headache, Johnny, and perhaps we
had better go and look at baby."

It was not often that Johnny complained, for he was a
wonderfully patient child; but to-day his habitual sage
stolidity seemed to have given way, and when he reached
the nursery he began to cry.

Twelve months ago Kate would have consigned him to
the care of his attendant, and gone down-stairs to the
parlor with a lady-like sense of annoyance; but now Barbara's responsibility seemed to have descended upon her
shoulders, and she exerted herself to her utmost in the
matter of consoling. She took Johnny upon her knee
and told him one of the always available stories; she sung
a little song for him; she built a bark house on the
hearth, and gravely related the history of its supposed

occupants. But though the tears stopped, Johnny was not himself. He could not be moved to laughter, even at the adventures of Jack the Giant Killer. He only sat still and listened, resting his head upon his hand, and now and then closing his eyes heavily. As she watched him Kate began to feel nervous, and at last she was positively frightened, for, as she ended her stories, he fell into a deep, unnatural sleep upon her arm. She laid her hand against his cheek and found it burning hot, and there was the same scarlet color on the skin which had alarmed her in baby.

"Aunt Dorcas," she said, quietly, "I will go downstairs and speak to Mr. Seymour about sending for the doctor. I am afraid these children are going to be ill."

There was a little decisive click in the manner of shutting the door behind her as she left the room. She was thinking how much oftener fate was going to compel her to put herself in Carl Seymour's way.

"From beggar to heiress, and from heiress to beggar!" she said, a thought bitterly. "And now I am mistress of a household, and sick nurse in prospective. What next?"

And then she tapped at the studio door, and a voice answered her summons with, "Come in."

Since morning, Carl had been shut up in his room,

working fiercely. The door opened, and he felt no little surprise at the sight of the slender, black-robed figure of the serene-eyed young lady, who stood quietly on the threshold, one slim, soft-looking hand resting upon the handle.

"I beg pardon for disturbing you," she said, gravely; "but I thought I ought to come and tell you that Johnny is not well, and baby is no better, and I should like to see the doctor."

At any rate, she did not commit herself in saying this lesson, for the purple-irised eyes met his gaze without a quiver of their fringes. He rose from his chair at once.

"I will see Dr. Chaloner myself," he said. "I am sorry to hear this. My sister will be so anxious. Is there anything I can do for you while I am out, Miss Davenant?"

"Nothing," she said, with a cold bow of thanks, and after a few more civil words, she left him as quietly as she had come.

"What a pleasant position!" she said, stopping in the hall a moment. "If it were not for the children I should leave the house to-morrow."

CHAPTER XIV.

AS TRUE AS STEEL.

JOHNNY was still sleeping when Kate re-entered the nursery, and as baby was fretting, she took the latter from aunt Dorcas and tried to pacify him.

She was still engaged in the somewhat trying occupation when Carl came in with the doctor, a jolly, good-humored, fatherly old gentleman, who was one of Barbara's special weaknesses.

Kate was conscious of an effort to look as if she was used to her position, but it was somewhat of a failure, despite her demurely upraised, questioning eyes, as he took the little one's hand in his.

"I hope it is nothing serious?" she asked, for his face had clouded, he being a doctor with an unprofessionally warm heart, and interested withal in sunny little Mrs. Armadale's olive-branches.

"Well," he said, slowly, "I hope not. There is another invalid, you say. I should like to see him."

His voice was so gravely doubtful that Kate felt

startled, and by the time he turned to her again, after looking at Johnny, she was absolutely pale.

"Mrs. Armadale is away from home, Mr. Seymour tells me. How long will she be absent?"

"Two weeks," replied Kate. "But we are expecting a letter from her this evening."

There was not much to be gleaned from the gentleman's grave "Ah!" and not much to be read in his face, as he wrote out his prescriptions and handed them to her.

"You have a seemingly experienced assistant," he said, glancing at aunt Dorcas. "For yourself, I should say this responsibility was a new one; but you must not allow yourself to be frightened," with a kindly smile.

"Then you think there is danger?" hesitatingly.

"Not at present. There may be. At any rate, it will be as well to send for Mrs. Armadale."

He spoke reassuringly, but in her quick, upward glance, Kate saw he had not told her all he feared; and when he had gone to the parlor to talk to Carl, she gave baby a tight little clasp that said a great deal. She had learned to love pretty Barbara so, and she had learned to see so clearly how these children were the affectionate little creature's very heart-strings, that she could not bear the idea of her coming back to find them in danger, or, perhaps (she thought it with a faint shiver), worse. At any rate, she would try to take her place and be faithful, and she bent down and kissed the tiny face again.

She was very busy all the evening, but she was not too busy to watch anxiously for the postman's arrival, and when he came she listened eagerly to the announcement of the letters. There might be one from Mrs. Armadale, and if so half her anxiety would be lifted off her mind.

"Mr. Armadale," said the man's voice. "Two for Mr. Seymour, two for Miss Davenant. That's all."

"Two for Miss Davenant!" she thought, wonderingly. "Where can the second be from?"

They were brought up to her soon after. One evidently from Barbara, the other a blue-enveloped epistle, with a commonplace business-like look about it that dispelled her curiosity.

"Looks like a circular of some kind," she said, indifferently. "People forget I am 'nothing but a governess;'" and she laid it aside carelessly and opened Barbara's envelope.

It was not a very long letter, and evidently written under pressure of some little mysterious excitement, but it was very affectionate and cheerful. Kate felt almost heart-sick when she saw how cheerful and free from doubt it was. Messages for Johnny and Clara, and kisses for the baby, love to Carl, and affectionate hopes that Kate would not find her position irksome.

That was all; and then came a sentence that made the poor girl actually grow pale with the renewed weight of her forebodings.

"I do not know where I shall be when you hear from me again. We leave Washington to-night, but have not decided on our route."

This was an unexpected blow. For, after what the doctor had said, Carl had resolved to telegraph to Washington for his sister. But now Barbara would be gone before the telegram could reach her. Nor could any telegram find her till she got to New Orleans. She dropped the letter from her hands with something like terror in her expression.

"What shall I do?" she said. "Oh! what shall I do if the children become worse?"

It seemed as if she was to be fairly shaken, for the next moment Johnny stirred in his bed with a little moaning cry. She got up and went to him and touched his forehead.

"Are you awake, Johnny?" she said, trying to speak cheerfully. "Don't you want to see mamma's letter?"

He gave a sharp turn, tossing his hands upward, and staring blankly into her face with a look that made her feel faint and sick.

"It is something terrible, I am sure," she said to aunt Dorcas, who was just entering. "I think I had better go and speak to Mr. Seymour again."

There was no one else she could speak to. She felt that in her sudden sense of terror, and she forgot everything but Barbara and Barbara's children as she went down-stairs to find Carl.

He had been reading the letters he had received, and had tossed them upon the table. He was standing upon the hearth, and as she came in he turned round sharply with a startled look at her anxious face.

She went to him, and took Barbara's letter out of her pocket.

"The postman brought me this letter from Mrs. Armadale," she said. "She left Washington yesterday, and says she does not know where they make their next stoppage. Oh! what shall we do? I am afraid the children are in danger. Johnny has awakened, and does not know me."

Even in his trouble he could not help but notice one little phrase she had used. What shall "we" do she had said; and when she had said it, she spoke as any other girl would have spoken who had felt a sense of reliance upon his greater strength in the hour of trial.

He read the letter to the end, and then handed it back to her.

"It is too late even to telegraph now," he said. "Great heaven! if anything should happen—"

"I don't see that we can do anything but hope for the best," she interrupted. "Aunt Dorcas is very faithful, and—and I will try—" and there she broke off, because the excitement had made her voice unsteady and she could not trust it.

The doctor had promised to call again late in the evening, and at eight o'clock he came and found Mrs. Armadale's "Juno" sitting by Johnny's bed, and bathing his small, hot hands with cologne.

What he thought of the matter may be gleaned from a remark he made to his wife on his return home.

"I like Junos, my dear," he said, "and I always liked this Juno in particular; but when I saw her watching that child with her handsome face, as tender as a pretty girl's, I wanted to kiss her. Mrs. Armadale's babies will be taken care of, I am sure of that."

After he had left the nursery bedroom he stopped, talking with Carl a short time in the hall; and when he had gone, Mr. Seymour sent a message up-stairs, to the effect that he should like to see Miss Davenant for a few minutes.

He stopped his impatient walk across the floor when she came, and offered her a chair.

"I cannot stay," she said, gravely. "You wanted to see me about—"

It seemed as if he wished to see what effect the words he spoke would have upon her, for he came and stood behind the chair, and laid his hands on its back, and looked at her with his cold, haughty eyes.

"I thought it only right to inform you that Dr. Chaloner has told me what this sickness appears to be. It is scarlet-fever, Miss Davenant, and there is great danger in it. Of course we cannot expect you to risk your life—"

She stopped him here, lifting her head proudly and coloring to her forehead.

"Thank you for your caution," she said, with a faint sting of bitterness in her tone. "I dare say you mean to be kind, but with your permission I will run the risk. Mrs. Armadale left her children in my care, and I mean to be true to the trust. I don't know what you think of

me, Mr. Seymour," turning suddenly, " but I am not
wholly heartless, and I love the children; and because I
love them I will try to take their mother's place." And
she turned round and went out of the room, and left him
standing alone.

It was not a very calm face, but still it was a sufficiently
steady one that she presented to aunt Dorcas' criticisms
when she went up-stairs again.

" It is more serious than I thought," she said. " The
children have scarlet-fever, aunty, and we must prepare
for some hard work."

CHAPTER XV.

THE PEBBLE IN THE POOL.

CLARA was sent down-stairs to remain in her uncle's care and be kept out of the way, for, as yet, she had complained of nothing serious, and they tried to hope that she would escape the infection.

Then Kate set about her tasks in prospective quietly. She bathed her face and hands with cologne, brushed her hair back into a great knot, and changed her dress for a light, cool wrapper. There are some women who do everything gracefully and without losing their self-possession. Kate Davenant was one of them. It is astonishing what a woman can and will do when her heart is in her work. In after days, Kate looked back at the dreary hours of danger and suffering that followed with a shudder, wondering how she had lived through them. It was no light responsibility and no light labor that fell into her unaccustomed hands then. Sometimes she sickened and grew faint under its burden, and needed all her strength of will and purpose to rouse herself to fitness for it.

For a week she never left the nursery bedroom, hardly daring to sleep in her anxiety. Johnny lay upon his bed, scorched with fever and wildly delirious, moaning for water sometimes and crying for his mother; baby wailed, and fretted, and slept by turns; and as a finishing stroke to all the evils, at the end of the week Clara dropped fainting on the parlor floor, and was brought up to the sick-room to be nursed with the rest. Here was a unique position for the Circe!

The day Clara was taken ill, Carl carried her up-stairs in his arms and stayed with her all night. When he first entered, Kate was sitting by Johnny, with baby lying across her shoulder, as she leaned her head wearily against the chair-back; and a fierce throb shook his heart as he noted her white face and the purple shadows round her eyes. Short as they were, those seven days had absolutely changed her. When he had left Dorcas with Clara, he came back into the nursery, feeling as if some force controlled him.

"Kate," he said, for he forgot everything in his new pity for her, and spoke as he would have spoken to Barbara, "you must leave Johnny to me, and go and sleep. Another week of such labor and watching will kill you."

Perhaps she had grown weak that his kindly tone

touched her so; at any rate, she glanced up at him with a softened smile.

"I could not go to sleep if I lay down," she said, trying to speak cheerfully. "I don't like to leave them for a moment. Look at Johnny's face," and she drew down the coverlid.

The poor little fellow's temples looked shrunken and hollow, a great scarlet spot blazed on each cheek, and his eyes were heavily closed.

"He has not spoken since yesterday." She did not care to control herself now, and the sudden tears choked her voice. "Oh! I wish Mrs. Armadale would come home!"

Carl looked down at the sweet, white face, thrilled to his very soul. There was something in it which he was beginning to understand, but which he had never understood before. Something of latent truth, something of what she had suffered, which now in her trouble was not hidden by any of the perfect acting. It was months since she had come to his house, and every day had been a slow step to the ending of the story. For months he had struggled with his fate, and now, as the soft eyes raised up to his and fell again, he felt that all the struggles, and bitterness, and contempt, were as nothing, and that he stood

to-night just where he had stood when their eyes met in
the little theatre at Newport, nearly four years ago. He
had tried to hate her, and learned to love her because her
sweet eyes were so tender; and as she stood there with
Barbara's baby in her arms, she seemed to blot out some
of the past, and her red lips drooped as little Kathleen's
might have done in such a womanhood as this. When
she had sung the pretty lullaby, his heart had wakened to
passionate regret and yearning; the one moment in which
her soft cheek had touched his breast had opened his eyes
to the truth; and now, in spite of himself and his pride,
he must needs speak a little of that truth in his remorse
for the times when he could see he had been cruel, if he
had been just.

"You must let me help you," he said. "You have
taken too heavy a burden upon yourself."

She looked up quickly, and then turned her face away.
She did not mean to repulse him, but there was a ring in
his voice that seemed almost a mockery, it recalled so
much to her. But, simple as the movement was, it stung
him.

"Cannot we forget the old wrongs for a while?" he
said, bitterly. "Or are we to be enemies forever?"

For a moment she hardly cared to raise her face, the red

had shot so sharply over its white. Like a man, he had misunderstood her, and, like a woman, she must hide her pain, so she answered him as bitterly as he had spoken.

"This is no time to remember wrongs," she said. "I don't want to remember them. I think we had better forgive each other till the children get well, Mr. Seymour." But as she spoke, great, hot tears leaped into her eyes, and stood there, and he saw them.

Just the pebble in the pool, but the ripples were circling to the shore.

For the last week the girl had been suffering through her whole being in her battle with herself and her re-awakened pain, but the stern necessity for self-control forced her to be strong where she might otherwise have been weak. She found no time to ask herself questions, and sometimes she was almost thankful for it.

From the evening that he brought Clara up-stairs in his arms, Carl Seymour gave her no chance to forget his presence in the house. Every day he was in the sick-room, sometimes bringing fruit, sometimes a few flowers; but, whatever his errand, always leaving behind him something of comfort, or hope, or rest for the sick nurse. Every action was quietly, almost coldly done; but, after a day or so, Kate began to notice, and was not sorry for

11

the evidence, that actual warfare was over. At any rate,
she said to herself, it was sympathy, and just then
sympathy, even from an enemy, would have been accept-
able. Once, as he passed through the room, he laid a
bunch of white flowers upon the table at her side. "They
will refresh you," he said, coolly, and then went on; and
she found herself gazing at them blankly, for they were
just such flowers as she had thrust aside when John
Crozier came to Newport. She went to smooth Clara's
pillow with a half sob rising in her throat, and suffocating
her.

"If Mrs. Armadale would come home," she would say
to herself. "If Mrs. Armadale would only come!"

And at last she made up her mind that when the
trouble was over, she would try her fortune at some far-
away place, where there were at least no ghosts to haunt
her.

But, in spite of everything, just what good had been
hidden and smothered in her worldliness, showed itself in
these days.

There was no time to act and diplomatize—no time to
feel bitter. What nothing else on earth could have done
the two weeks of unromantic labor did—made these two
enemies forget the fierce smart of self-contempt and old

regret. They were drawn together because they could not possibly have kept apart. Because she was compelled to rely upon him and trust to his assistance, Kate learned to shut her eyes calmly to everything that could have made the compulsory intercourse unpleasant. Because she must rely upon him, and he upon her, and, perhaps, for other reasons, Carl forgot his wrongs. Still it was nearly two weeks before anything of the truth reached the surface.

It was late one evening, and as she sat by the fire, with baby on a pillow on her lap, Carl found himself watching her and wondering. He was trying to call to mind the Circe with the dangerous eyes and scarlet cheeks, who had laughed at Tom Griffith; the Circe who had coldly used her fascinations and her beauty because it pleased her to outdo other women. It was not easy to place the two side by side and call them by one name, they seemed so far apart.

Would she live the same life again if Fortune turned the chances toward her? Would she amuse herself with her human bagatelle-board, as she had done before, and forget everything else? Just now, as the firelight struck on the glitter of her bent head, and danced over the shadows of her black dress, it showed her dreaming eyes full of wistfulness, and the old, cold, graceful scorn swept away.

She did not know at first that he was looking at her, she was so full of thought; but in a few minutes some magnetic influence made her turn toward him quickly, and meeting his eyes, she colored, hardly knowing why. Just as swiftly as she had looked up she looked down again. She had grown afraid of herself lately, and did not care to trust her face to his scrutiny. Then there was a long silence—such a long silence that she thought its stillness would force her to speak.

He had come into the nursery to look at the children, and he was leaning his elbow upon the mantel and gazing down at her. What was he thinking of? she asked herself, impatiently. What was he going to say? She felt as if she was waiting for something.

And so she was, unconsciously, it appeared, for suddenly he drew something from his pocket and held it out to her without speaking a word. Her first glance at it made her start, and then the red deepened and glowed upon her skin until cheeks and forehead burned hot. It was a slender gold chain. The firelight glittered on it as it was suspended from his hand, and a little onyx cross hung to it—a little Gothic cross, tipped with gold.

The ripples were very near the shore then.

She hardly knew what to say, and an exclamation broke forth almost unconsciously.

"You kept it?" she said.

He bent his head.

"It dropped from your neck and caught upon my coat when you fell. I kept it because— Well, it was yours, and you wore it at Newport, Kate."

How near the ripples were!

She took it from his outstretched hand, her own trembling in spite of herself, and in spite of herself again, another question leaped out.

"Was it because I wore it at Newport that you kept it?"

"Yes," he said, with a faint echo of bitterness in his voice. "It is not so easy to forget, you see."

Proud man as he was, bitter, and cruel, and harsh as he had been, her tender eyes and tender voice touched his innermost soul, and shook its strength.

I said before, that once conquered, this man was conquered wholly and forever. And if you, my reader, could have seen the pallor of his haughty face, you would have acknowledged that I spoke truly.

She held the chain for a moment, looking at it, and then she extended it to him again.

"I will not take it from you if you would like to keep it. We have both said hard words to each other, Mr. Seymour, but we have been friends for a week now, and I, for one, am not inclined to break the truce."

She smiled up into his eyes as she said it, and tried to speak carelessly; but it was a hard struggle that helped her to maintain her self-possession.

"Do you mean this?" he asked her.

She bent her head, still holding out the chain, with the Circe's smile.

"Why not?"

He took it and began to wind it round his fingers.

"You are a true woman," he said, "and so are wise. I am a true man, and so not wise. Since you have been here I have said things to you which had better have been left unsaid. Try to forget them." And he turned on his heel and went out of the room without another word.

If her position had seemed hard to her before, it seemed harder now. Woman-like, she would have gone along smoothly without a passing hint of the undercurrent; but he, with exasperating masculine pertinacity, must needs touch the half-healed wounds, perhaps feeling some aggrandizement in his own pain. Blame him, if you like—call him a weak fool; I have only one thing to say

—he loved her. If you are a man, and have some time loved a woman, you will understand how he might act madly; if you are a woman, and have ever loved, you will forgive him for it.

Carl went to his room that. night not to sleep, but to hold that glittering chain upon his finger, and look at it, to sneer at himself, and call himself hard names, and then to ponder over the pretty picture he had left behind him in the nursery.

CHAPTER XVI.

THE RIPPLES CIRCLE TO THE SHORE.

IT was daylight before Kate left her seat at the fire where she had sat dreaming. Toward morning Johnny fell asleep, and baby seemed better, and at aunt Dorcas' decisive command, Kate relinquished her post, and lay down. She passed the mirror as she went to the couch, and caught a glimpse of herself. She shrugged her shoulders a little at the white face and shadowy eyes. Her belt ribbon had actually grown loose, and she fancied she saw faint lines round her mouth. What had brought them there? Anxiety, perhaps, and perhaps, something else. Well, it could not last forever; and after this was all over, she could go away and make up her mind to settle down into a middle-aged woman.

"There are women who lead such lives," she said. "Ah, me! I suppose I have done with the rest, but I can't quite reconcile it with the Circe. Whose fault is it, though?" She asked herself the question, sharply, and then as sharply turned away and went to the couch and lay down, burying her face in the cushions.

The doctor came again early in the morning, and after looking at his patients, announced a decided improvement.

"What is the matter with you?" he asked, turning upon Kate. "If you were any one else, I should say you had been crying all night like a baby."

She shook her head with a faint smile.

"But I am not any one else," she said, "and I don't cry—often. I am only tired."

But, shall I tell you, reader, that there was a little hypocrisy in her quiet face, for if she had not cried like a baby, at least she had lain awake with an uncomfortable throb in her throat, and hot tears starting now and then to her eyes, because the little cross, glittering in the firelight, and the haughty, cynical face seemed to taunt her so.

"Try to forget them," he had said, and in saying it, had brought back to her everything of remembrance.

"If Mrs. Armadale would only come home," she said over to herself: and that day her wish was realized. She hardly knew why, but toward evening she began to feel somewhat more hopeful. The children seemed quieter, and, for one thing, Mr. Seymour had kept his room, and she had regained her composure, and she found herself looking back over the three weeks as something which was almost a thing of the past. It was four o'clock, and she had just taken her place by Johnny, when one of the servants came to the door looking not a little flurried.

"If you please—" she began, and then stopped.

Kate looked up as she fed Johnny with a spoonful of jelly.

"What is the matter?" She was not easily frightened, and spoke quite composedly.

"There's a carriage coming up the drive, ma'am," said the girl, "and we think maybe it's Mrs. Armadale."

Kate laid her glass and spoon down, it must be confessed, with a sudden leap of the heart. What if they had not received any of the telegrams or letters, and were coming home to meet the news as a shock.

"Lie down, Johnny," she said, and left the room and went down-stairs just in time to meet Carl coming out of the parlor.

"They are coming," he said, anxiously. "I wonder if they received our letters?"

"I shall meet them at the door," said Kate, decidedly. "If Mrs. Armadale does not know, I think I can best tell her myself."

But she was spared the task, for in three minutes the carriage had stopped, and poor little Mrs. Armadale almost burst from it, her pretty, young face perfectly deathly.

"Oh, Kate!" she said, in a little storm of self-reproaching sobs. "Oh, Kate! we never knew till Wednesday, on our way back from New Orleans, when we had an old telegram at Augusta, and—and tell me the worst."

"It is not so very bad," said Kate, following her, for she was actually on her way to the nursery before she had finished speaking. "They had the fever only in a mild form, and baby was very much weakened. I don't think there is any danger now."

But Barbara had rushed into the sick-room, and was bending over the cradle, trying in vain to choke back her sobs as she lifted her little one in her arms.

"I—I can't help it," she said to Kate. "Oh! my poor little babies!" And then she was kissing Johnny and crying softly over him, and patting Clara's pillow and petting her, and talking to Kate, all at once. "What should I have done without you?" she said. "How can I thank you? And, oh! my best, patient dear, look at your pale cheeks!"

After her excitement was quieted somewhat, she insisted on wrapping Kate in a soft shawl, and making her lie down on the sofa to rest.

To tell the truth, now that the burden of responsibility was taken from her, this before unconquered Kate began to feel tired, and when she was fairly ensconced on the sofa, fell asleep, and slept with most unheroic soundness.

It was late when she awakened, and by the light of the fire she saw Barbara sitting by her in the rocking-chair, rocking to and fro, and evidently waiting impatiently for her awakening.-

"I am glad you have finished your sleep," she said, "I am so impatient to talk everything over. Kate, what *did* you think when you got Alf's letter? I always told him it would turn out so. It is like a romance, only there was so little mystery about it. They say Mr. Davenant was killed on the spot. He had always been a fast man, you know—"

Miss Davenant sat up in her lounge with a little extra color on her cheeks, and not a little extra beating at her heart. What did all this mean?

"I beg your pardon, Mrs. Armadale," she said; "but I don't understand. I never received any letter from Mr. Armadale. I never—"

Barbara broke in upon her.

"You don't understand?" she echoed. "You never received a letter? Alf wrote to you the day we left Washington."

Just then, and not till then, did something of remembrance flash across Kate's mind. What about the envelope she had laid aside and forgotten in her anxiety? She got up and went to the mantel-piece. Yes, there it was, just as she had left it, without breaking the seal. She did not sit down, she stood up just where she was, and tore it open and glanced at the signature, "Alfred Armadale;" and then she read the letter through. When she had finished, she looked up at Barbara, blood in her cheeks rising redly, a great flash of something in her eyes. At last! at last! Fortune had turned the tables once more. Her father's brother, who had never even seen her, had died from a fall from his horse; died without children and without a will; and she was his heir. Oddly enough, the thought that rose highest in the tumult of her mind was the most commonplace of thoughts. She was not to be a middle-aged governess, after all; she was not to grow old, and bitter, and faded, over music-lessons and French grammars. Mercenary this, of course; but permit me to say it was very natural. If she wished now she might go away from this terrible galling and humiliation, and, perhaps, forget it all.

"I never read this letter before," she said to Barbara. "I was so anxious that I laid it down and forgot it. I

don't know what to say. I can hardly believe it is true.
My uncle was so angry with pa for wronging ma that he
would never even see me."

Barbara got up quietly and went to her, and kissed her
on both cheeks.

"I hope it will make you happy, my dear," she said.
"I must congratulate you, but I cannot congratulate
myself. I shall lose my friend and my governess."

Twice in four years had Fate flung a golden grape into
Kate Davenant's hands. The first time it had only added
fresh bitterness to her lot; this second time it brought her
relief, not happiness.

Mr. Davenant was dead—killed by a fall from a wild,
unmanageable horse; and whether she deserved it, or not,
Miss Davenant was an heiress, again representing substan-
tially twenty thousand a year and two establishments.

There was no excitement in her manner as she sat by
Mr. Armadale, at the table in the library that night,
and entered into the particulars of her business. Her face
was quite calm and business-like, and while she listened to
his statements and replied to his inquiries, she was playing
with a pen-holder, and smiling now and then faintly.
Mr. Armadale had heard all the points of the case, and
only some few legal formalities must be gone through
before she could take possession.

It was ten o'clock before their work was finished, and then the gentleman congratulated her warmly.

Seymour had been sitting with them reading, and as his brother-in-law spoke, he glanced up quickly and looked at Miss Davenant.

She was standing by the table, resting one hand upon it, and toying with the pen-holder, her downcast eyes a little thoughtful. The bright lamplight was concentrated upon her, and showed the white-browed patrician face, and Clytie head, poised half haughtily, half carelessly. Her long, black dress made her look white and slender with its sombre heaviness; the great waves of burnished hair were twisted in a massive knot on the slim, shapely neck, and there was a deep scarlet spot on either cheek. She was a beautiful woman, as much the Circe as ever; she was a beautiful picture, and the touching tenderness of her smile made her dazzling.

"Does money make people happy?" she asked, lifting her soft eyes. "If it does, you know I shall be happy, for I can buy twenty thousand dollars worth of happiness every year. But then if it *don't*, I might only be a rich heiress, after all, in spite of your kind wish—and the thousands."

She only spoke half seriously; but when she ended, her

voice shook a little in the face of her smiles, and there was a touch of truth in the almost imperceptible tremor of her red lower-lip, that filled the man with a mad longing to go to her and wind his arm around her waist, and quench the pride in her proud face with kisses that should force her heart to speak truly. But men don't do these things, you know, and he could only look at her a little longer, wondering if her sweet eyes had made a madman of him.

She came to the fire when she had done with Mr. Armadale, and stood upon the hearth, resting her arched foot on the fender, in her favorite fashion, and smiling upon him with the Circe's witchery. She was free now, you see; no longer a dependant or menial; perhaps, after a month's time, they might never meet again—and, besides, she could afford it. Her thousands had bought her that right, at least.

"Won't you congratulate me, Mr. Seymour?" she asked. "Or do you think I am a better nurse than heiress? I want to hear you say you are glad for my sake."

"Which must I congratulate you upon first?" he said. "Your happiness, or your riches, or both at once?"

"For both at once. The riches are to buy the happiness, you know. How much shall I get for twenty thousand dollars, I wonder?"

"A great deal, I hope," he answered her. "I congratulate you with all my heart, Miss Davenant."

She went out of the room directly afterward, and the last glimpse he caught of her face, as she closed the door, showed him the faint smile lying round her lips still; but when she stood in the hall alone it faded, and the lights of the swinging-lamp swam a little through the mist over her eyes, and when she went slowly up the broad stair-case it was gone altogether, and there was nothing but a faint curve upon the red mouth.

It seemed as if Barbara's presence acted upon her children like a spell, for, from the time she kissed and cried over them, they recovered gradually.

"But how can I ever thank Kate?" said Barbara, to her husband and Mr. Seymour. "Dorcas says she never left them for an hour; and Dr. Chaloner told me that she saved baby just with her never-tiring care. It is so odd how naturally a woman loves children: but then Kate is so good."

And even during the recovery, Kate's goodness did not diminish. She would stay with Mrs. Armadale until everything was arranged, she said; and then, when the

12

invalids were better, they must come and help her to take
possession of her own country-seat.

"You must get married," said Alf. "You ought to be
married, Miss Davenant."

She laughed at him with brilliant cheeks, and lifted her
arched, brown brows.

"Ought! Why, Mr. Armadale? Do I need somebody
to manage me, or somebody to manage?"

"You need both," laughed Alf. "You have relied
upon yourself too long, and you want a master!"

Mr. Seymour did not say very much; but, speaking
truly, this young lady who "needed a master," was not
comfortable in his presence. Her delicate skin had a trick
of flaming suddenly and hotly under his glance; and her
eyelids were too apt to lower and droop when he spoke;
so, whenever it was possible, she kept out of his way.
Toward him she was brilliant, and dazzling, and fascinating; just as she had been at Newport, only now holding
her heart in a leash with something of shame. He loved
her, she knew; he had not forgiven her, she thought; he
could not respect her, she was sure: accordingly, she must
sneer herself down, and so she tried hard to do it—with
just such success as might be expected.

CHAPTER XVII.

LOST AND FOUND,

ONE day she actually went into her room and lighted a wax-taper, so that she might burn the souvenirs in her desk. And when she had taken them out and looked at them, (she did not attempt to read them,)—guess what she did?

She bent over them with flaming cheeks, almost unconciously, lower, lower, until her soft lips touched a card with Carl's name written upon it, and then she started back and pushed them aside angrily and crushed them together, and locked them in the drawer again, and after blowing out the taper, left the room. She *dare* not do it! She had found her master, and now, after conquering and scorning others, had come to the bitter sense of scorning herself.

It was a month before the business was fairly settled, and by that time Kate said she was tired of it.

Davenant Place was ready for her reception, wrote the late owner's steward, and many things required her presence there. Did she want the green-houses kept up? What was to be done with the horses?

"I suppose I had better go," said the young lady, twisting the note in her fingers, and shrugging her graceful shoulders; and accordingly she began to make her preparations. Was she sorry? She said so to Mrs. Armadale, when that lady talked to her about her prospects; she said so to Mr. Armadale; she said so to the children, who were now convalescent. She did not say so to Carl. She told him she was going, and laughed a little, triumphant laugh, as if she enjoyed the idea of her power in prospective. She was sitting in the parlor, leaning back in the very chair she had sat in the first evening of her arrival, and her fair hands were crossed idly on her lap, when they talked about it first.

"I *am* glad," she said. "I wanted the money, and I have got it. I love Mrs. Armadale, and I love the children; but I did not want to be a governess all my life. Was that wrong?" she asked, with a sudden bright lifting of her face to his, which was just such an audacious piece of acting as no other woman would have dared, for all the while she was faint and sick at heart.

No, he thought not. How could it be wrong? And then he looked at her, and her cheeks grew hot, and she

She was not going to be a belle, she told Mrs. Armadale, she was going to be Lady Bountiful, and nurse the sick, and make flannel night-caps for rheumatic pensioners; so her preparations need not be extensive, and besides, she wanted to make the most of her time. So, when her trunks were packed, she nursed baby and talked nonsense to him, and told Johnny stories, and sung little songs for Clara, generally ending with a faint mist over her eyes. And Carl, sitting in his studio, heard her sweet voice in the nursery, and the rustle of her robes in the passages, and having heard, flung his brush aside, and hid his face upon his folded arms with a bitter pang.

"It might have been!" he said. "Ah, Kathleen! Mavourneen! Mavourneen!"

How they would miss her! They all found it out, and talked about it, and, listening to them, he wakened to the stern truth that he loved her still, and should miss her, too; and when she was gone the whole house would seem lonely to him.

As for her, she was almost glad that the time had come when the ghosts might be exorcised. She grew feverish and impatient, and sometimes wakened at night, startled and nervous, and lay sleepless, wondering wearily how long her life would be, and if there would come no change in it, and if she would live and grow old, a rich, lonely woman to the end. She would try to be kind, she thought, vaguely, and Barbara, and Barbara's children, should come and stay with her, and she would help them to enjoy their innocent lives with her grand, lonely house, and her riches.

And then she supposed she would get old and faded, and there would be an end of life at last. But in some way, generally, at this conclusion (being twenty-three, and a woman) she forgot her philosophy, and felt impatient, even while she did not allow herself to ask what the impatience meant.

About three nights before their expected separation, Mrs. Armadale's governess came into the nursery for a final chat. Every one had retired, and after undressing to go to bed, Miss Davenant came into the room. A large, soft-looking scarlet shawl was wrapped round her, which was by no means brighter-colored than her soft cheeks; and she had loosened her hair, and was going to fasten it up for the night.

"I wanted to talk a little," she said, with a sigh; so she seated herself on a low chair by the fire. "I—I don't know quite how it is, but I feel rather egotistical to-night. I want to talk about myself."

"Then talk, please," said Mrs. Armadale. "I am sure I shall be glad to hear. What is it?"

There was a short silence, in which Miss Davenant twisted a great shining roll of hair round her fingers, and looked into the fire meditatively.

"I don't know," she said, at last, with a soft little laugh, that sounded like a soft little sob. "I wonder if you could tell me, Mrs. Armadale?"

Barbara's eyes were raised slowly and fixed with a keen inquiry upon the fair face.

"Kate, my dear," she said, in her affectionate voice, "I think you can tell best yourself."

Kate glanced up quickly.

"You remember what I told you once before," she said. "I mentioned no names, for I could not betray others. Well, it is the same story over again. I am tired of myself. I don't know what to do with myself."

Barbara laid her hand upon the girl's arm.

"You told me something else," she said, softly. "You told me that you had done a great wrong in doing what you did; you said that you had loved the man you wronged better than any one else. Is it quite out of your power to repair the wrong you did?"

She did not answer at first. Her heart beat fast and impatiently.

"I never can repair it!" she said, lacing the heavy scarlet fringe of her shawl through her fingers. "A woman may not speak as a man may. Because I am a woman, I must keep my penitence to myself. I am unhappy, and I must profess to be happy. What a life we women lead!"

"You said your romance ended four years ago," began Barbara again, after a pause.

"Yes," in a low voice; "four years ago."

"When—when you were at Newport?"

"Yes."

Both pairs of eyes raised softly and met with a flash; then one pair drooped, and Kate turned her head away.

It was some minutes before they spoke again, and then the conversation seemed to flag a little.

Barbara's heart was full to the brim. Just the one quick, upward glance had told her all, and there seemed nothing more to be said. Still the clock struck twelve before they separated. As the last chime rung out upon the stillness, Miss Davenant rose from her seat and wound the scarlet shawl round her white-robed form. Then she stopped before Mrs. Armadale, a trifle hesitatingly.

"I want to say something to you before I go away," she said, in a low voice. "I want to thank you for something. Mrs. Armadale, when I came here first I was bitter, and worldly, and disappointed. I had met with nothing but selfishness and scheming—and I was selfish and scheming myself. I don't think I had seen the fair side of life. I did not expect to be happy, I only expected to earn my salary like a servant, and hold my own, because my pride helped me. I had no mother to take care of me," her voice faltered a little, "and so I was obliged to take care of myself. But when I came here it seemed as if my eyes were opened. You were happy, and your husband was happy, and so were your children; and yet, when you married Mr. Armadale, you had forgotten everything but that you loved him. I am twenty-three years old, Mrs. Armadale," her voice dropped, and broke down into a tremor of passionate sobs. "I am twenty-three years old, and you are the first woman who has loved me, and kissed me, because I was a girl and lonely. I shall never forget it—I never can forget. You have shown me how happy a good woman may be. I want to thank you for being kind to me."

Both Barbara's arms were folded round her, and Barbara's soft cheek was pressed against hers. It seemed as if the loving little creature's heart was full almost to breaking.

"Oh, my dear!" she said, between her kindly kisses, "if I have ever made you feel less lonely, how happy I am! I loved you always from the first, and I tried to think of you as if you had been my own little Clara grown into a woman. I hope you will be happy, and I think you will. In the end, perhaps, I shall see you some good man's wife, lóving your husband, and loving your children, and thanking God. I hope I shall, my dear, I hope I shall!" And she held the fair face a little from her, and kissed it again and again.

The next day passed quietly, one might say dully, and, at last, when evening came, Mr. Armadale and his wife, and Carl and Kate were in the parlor, talking by the fire-light.

"Don't let us have any other light," said Miss Davenant. "Darkness suits my mood this evening."

She was restless and excited. Barbara had never seen her so brilliant before, and looked at her scarlet cheeks uneasily.

She sat in the red glow of the fire, talking to them just as she only could talk, flinging out flashes of graceful non-sense and wit that were almost dazzling. There was a vein of sarcasm through it all which was bewitching, in spite of its being sarcasm; and she looked so like the

Circe, with her delicate flushes and great purple eyes, her soft voice, and her wonderful smile, that Carl found himself startled, and listened to her with something like a pang. She sneered a little—half as though she was in jest—at her experience; and she was not afraid to laugh, as she acknowledged how the world had cheated her.

It was late when they all retired; at least all, to speak correctly, but Carl, who, left to himself, drew his chair nearer the fire and bent over it, pondering in the dead silence. She was going away to-morrow, and then all would be over. The pictured face up-stairs had smiled upon him from its frame as he went out of the door, and there was a fancy in his mind now that he would hide the pictures out of sight, and leave his home to Barbara and her children, and go away to try and fill his life with travel and hard work. The sight of Kate's sweet face had tortured him, but the loss of it would drive him mad.

He had been sitting alone half an hour, with these thoughts making themselves half distinct to his mind, when he heard some one coming down-stairs softly, and then the door swung open and Miss Davenant entered, evidently thinking the room unoccupied. She had come down on an unexpected errand, it appeared. The scarlet had left her cheeks, and in contrast with the heavy

sombreness of her dark, sweeping purple, she looked wonderfully like the marble Clytie in her whiteness.

She came to the table, and after some searching took up
a little volume, and then it was that she caught sight of
Carl and turned round.

"I beg your pardon," she said, with a slight start. "I
did not expect to find any one here. I came for a book I
left."

She approached the hearth as she spoke, evidently with
something of effort to retain her self-possession, and as the
red light struck upon her, he saw there were faint shadows round her eyes, and a heaviness as of tears upon the
lashes.

"The book is an old favorite of mine," she said; "and
as I was locking my trunks I missed it. I leave to-
morrow, you know."

"So soon?" he asked; and then, as if unconsciously,
extended his hand for the book.

It was a pretty edition of Longfellow's "Evangeline,"
and he had read extracts from this same volume to her at
Newport. One day he remembered—for how could he
forget?—they had walked to the Spouting Rock together,
and talked, as a man and woman will talk, of the heroine's
fidelity; and now he thought he could almost see her face

again, as she smiled and told him that none but a woman could have been so true. He hardly knew why, but he began to turn over the leaves slowly, with a half-defined wish to find the extract he had read.

There was a moment of silence after he had said "So soon;" but at last it was broken by a restless movement on Kate's part, and he looked up at her. She was haughty, and, perhaps, a thought cold; but if she could have undone the past she would have undone it; and now, as they must part, it might be forever, she wanted to make him what reparation she could. She had defied him before, and tried to humiliate him, and her worldly experience taught her that a man's worst grief is his humiliation, and so she tried to make his somewhat less bitter and complete. If she had been only Mrs. Armadale's governess, the words would never have been spoken; but now she was free to dare to say them, and he could not see more in them than a proud woman humbled a little through her very pride's intensity.

"Yes," she said, in a low voice, "I am going away to-morrow. We have not been very good friends while we have been together, Mr. Seymour, but I don't want to leave an enemy behind me. I did you a great wrong four years ago, and—and I deserve any bitter thought you may have of me. I wanted to say this to you before I go away, because—because—because—"

Her voice faltered—shook—stopped. Carl had turned over the leaves of the book as he listened to her, and just at the end something had slipped from its pages and fallen upon the carpet. A scrap of sea-weed it was, dry and brown, and tied with a bit of silver cord in a lover's knot. So insignificant it looked, so worthless; but it broke down the barriers of years.

He had picked it up from the sands that day at the Spouting Rock, and laid it in the book to mark the passage. She had laughed, and broken the cord from her glove, and tied it in the quaint, old-fashioned knot, jestingly saying she would keep it as a souvenir, and showing it to him years after, would prove she had been a faithful —friend.

"Friend," she had said, but the swift down-droop of her eyes had said more, and he had kissed her gloved hand as answer.

Ah, me! how fiercely the two hearts beat as it came to light again, with its freight of memory, and the faint scent of the salt sea about it! One moment she flushed, the next she paled, and then she stood still and waited to see what would come of it, every throb of her heart seeming like a great wrench.

He stooped down, white to the lips, picked it up, and then looked at her a moment in silence.

"You kept it?" he said, at last.

The very words she had used to him, but his voice was fairly hoarse.

It seemed as if she had staked all for nothing. She had acted her part for months, and now a little brown sea-weed had shown that it was acting, and humbled her pride to the dust. It was no use now. She might as well tell the truth.

"Yes," she answered him. "I kept it, Mr. Seymour," and then she turned her face away.

He got up from his seat, and went to her just as he had done that last day at Newport.

"Why?" he said.

The power lay in his hands now, and their places had changed.

She did not answer; she only looked up at him with her beautiful eyes.

"Tell me," he said again. "Tell me why?"

Then her pride, and resentment, and humiliation broke forth.

"It was yours," she said, passionately, bitterly. "You gave it me at Newport when we were both better than we

are now. I have not forgotten, either. That is why.
Now let me go!" And she tried to wrench her hands
away from his grasp.

But he held them fast—fast and hard, in a sort of fierce
despair.

"Are we never to forgive each other?" he cried. "Can
we never forgive each other? There is a picture up-stairs
with a childish, innocent face. I loved you when you
were that child, Kate; I loved you when you grew to be a
woman; I have loved you all my life, and—and you will
either save my soul or ruin it. Let us try to forget the
wrong we have done. Let us try to make the future more
unselfish than the past has been. Be my wife, and so help
me to regain what I have lost of heaven. Lift your sweet
face to me—I want to see it! Oh! if the past has been
only a dream, Kathleen! Mavourneen! Mavourneen!"

He clasped her in his arms as if she had been a child;
he drew her head upon his breast; he pushed the heavy
hair back, and kissed eyes, and cheeks, and lips, as none
but a man who had lost and found a love could have done.

And she—this Circe, who for the first time in her
twenty-three years of life had found her true place—flung
all aside, and spoke as a woman will speak when her heart
conquers her and forces her to be generous. They had

suffered and been wrong, but her kisses bridged the old gulf, and made the suffering a thing forever dead.

"Forgive!" she echoed. "It was he who must forgive! It was he who must forget! Could it ever be? Could he trust her again?" Between her sobs she said it; between his kisses and tender words; and fresh kisses were his answer.

And then he sat down again, still with his arms clasped around her, and she knelt upon the hearth with her beautiful face hidden upon his breast, and drooping.

"Fourteen years!" she said, at last, "nearly fourteen years! If we could bring them back again and make them better! If we could bring back what we have lost!"

When a man loves a woman truly, there is but one thing in his life—that one thing is his love, all bears upon it, he has only one answer to all her words—that answer is, "I love you." So it was with Carl Seymour.

"Lost!" he echoed. "Never lost! Sad as those years have been they have brought you to me, Mavourneen! My darling! Mine!"

It was a long time before she told him John Crozier's story; but it was told at last.

"I was ill for a long time after you left Newport," she

13

said. "They thought I was dying, and I hoped I was. But I got better, and I was so wretched that even my aunt, at last, advised me to break the engagement. Let us never speak of it again. Love me, and try to trust me; but let us never, never look back upon that, the thought of it would make you love me less. Promise me," and she lifted her face.

And then he promised, and put love's ancient seal upon the pledge, a little reverently, and with such tenderness, that she knew that at last she was loved as a woman must be loved, as every woman should be loved, with a true heart and a great strength, and a faith as pure and perfect as a child.

CHAPTER XVIII.

SAFE AT LAST.

BARBARA bent over baby's cradle, and went on singing softly, looking up at Kate.

Kate had been late this morning, and when she came into the sunshiny room, there was a soft rose-red on her cheeks, and the look of happy tears in her purple eyes.

Barbara knew what was coming. Barbara was a woman, and did not say much at first, she only sang over baby, and rocked the cradle with her pretty foot, and waited.

Kate loitered over the flower-stand for a while and tried to talk, but at last she came into the deep, sunny window to Barbara, and stood there trifling with a late flower, the crimson fluttering softly on her face, and her lips a little parted.

"Did you find the 'Evangeline?'" asked Barbara, innocently, at last.

Miss Davenant's eyes lifted, and flashed through their veil of tears—she was so happy.

"Yes," she said. "And I found something else!"

Barbara's nonsense melted into an April shower.

"I know all about it," she said, softly. "Carl has told me. It makes me very happy. God has been good to you, my darling;" and she kissed her again. Just then the little one stirred in the cradle, and cooed, and caught at the sunbeams streaming through the window, just as children of a larger growth grasp at life's glitter; and Kate Davenant turned her face to the sunshine, too, with the tremor of last night's kisses upon her lips.

"God has been very good to me," she cried. "I think he has made me a child again, little Kathleen, 'Kathleen Mavourneen' once more!"

THE END.

Printed in the United States
98207LV00002B/26/A